SURVIVE THE PAST

TOBY J NICHOLS

SEVERED PRESS
HOBART TASMANIA

SURVIVE THE PAST

CHAPTER 1

Jack squinted against the setting sun. It glanced off the water in blinding ripples. The three guys and one girl out on the jet skis didn't seem to care that it was getting late as they cut across the sea. Jack leaned on the railing and watched them.

His job was entertainment, and supervision, as well as general cleaning. Emma was the chef and Paul drove the boat. He couldn't see either of them from where he was. No doubt Emma was making dinner. His stomach grumbled just thinking about it, but he'd have to secure everything before he ate— not with the guests, obviously.

He lifted his gaze from the water to scan the horizon. There were plenty of other boats still out on the water. From other private yachts to cruise liners to fishing vessels. He glanced up at the darkening sky flickered with green.

He'd heard the warnings about increasing solar flare activity, but like most people he wasn't bothered. A few people were warning that this time was different because there was increased movement from the magnetic poles.

Laughter dragged his attention back to the guests. At least they were laughing now. The first day had been argument filled and Jack had half expected the older of the two brothers to demand they return to port. He hadn't, but probably only because his girlfriend had pouted.

Jack forced a smile as the guests made their way back to the boat. He helped them dock and climb off. They tossed their life vests on the deck and moved on like he didn't exist. The younger brother, Oliver, glanced back. For a moment Jack thought he was going to say something, but then his friend grabbed his arm and dragged him away.

It was easier if he didn't exist to them. They didn't live in the same world. He sighed and stowed the life jackets, then checked that the skis were secure.

He knew from the arguments that Oliver was supposed to have brought his girlfriend, but they had broken up and so he'd brought his best friend instead.

Jack knew far more about the breakup, the ex, and the brothers than he needed to. Sure, he was friendly and polite, but that was part of the service. He enjoyed being out on the water and this job paid him to do that. Next year he'd have his ticket to captain, and his pay would go up accordingly. So he wasn't going to fuck it up by telling this bunch of spoiled, cashed up college students, only a few years younger than him, that he didn't care about their dramas.

No, he'd go out of his way to make sure they had a good time.

He double checked everything, then made his way up to where Paul sat in the bridge. "You can take us in for the night now."

Paul held up his finger to silence Jack. "Say again?"

The radio crackled and Jack checked the sky again. It rippled with green. An aurora over the Mediterranean from the increased solar flare activity. He shivered. It had been happening all week and was still unnerving. Tonight it was vivid.

"A whale?" Paul grinned. "Thanks for the tip, we'll check it out."

Jack rolled his eyes. While he was sure the guests would love it, it would take them longer to get back to port for the night. "Really?"

"Yeah, added value. It will only take ten minutes. Go and tell them."

Not go and ask, because of course they were going to say yes. Who wouldn't? When Jack had first started crewing on the yacht, he'd been as excited as anyone to see whales and dolphins up close. After four years, the novelty had worn off.

"What do you make of that?" Jack pointed out the window at the aurora.

"Everything still works, so it can't be that bad. Besides, it will keep it light for a bit longer so the guests can see the whale."

Jack took the hint and went to do Paul's bidding.

Oliver and his friend Noah were sitting in their shorts, drinking beer in the galley. The brother and girlfriend were missing. No prizes for guessing why.

"Want to see a whale up close?" Jack put on his best perky, excited host voice.

Oliver shrugged, then grinned. "Sure. I'll let Henry know."

***

Oliver watched as Jack walked out of the galley, then lifted his eyebrow at Noah, his supposed best friend. They'd been dating for the best part of six months, and he hadn't found a way to tell Henry that he'd broken up with his girlfriend until it was far too late to back out of this holiday. After the scene Henry had made about the cruise now being uneven—too many men and not enough women—Oliver wasn't about to confess the truth.

He'd been watching Jack since he'd first gotten on the boat. There was something about him, maybe it was that he was calm no matter what and that he could ignore Henry's barbs, which only annoyed Henry further, that drew his attention. Since then, he'd been trying to figure out what Jack's deal was. Sometimes it seemed like he was watching him and Noah a little too much, which had given him an idea. He'd mentioned it to Noah while they were on the ski.

"Totally." Noah nodded. "Do you want me to ask?"

"Do you think he would?" Oliver's pulse quickened, and he wasn't sure if it was from excitement or fear.

Noah scrunched his nose. "Probably not."

Even though they often joked about what it would be like to have a third, they had never done it. He'd nearly convinced his ex-girlfriend to give it a go, but he'd been too shit scared that she'd realize it was because he wanted the extra dick. Then he'd met Noah.

"I'd better bang on the door." And hopefully ruin the good time for both of them. Oliver took his beer and thumped on the suite his brother and girlfriend were sharing. "Hey, there's a whale if you want to see it."

He thought he heard his brother groan. Oliver bit back a laugh and made his way back to the deck so he could see the whale. Noah was already up there, chatting to Jack. He was going to die if Noah had said anything. Oliver's skin heated, and he blamed it on the sunburn from being out on the water all day.

They were moving further from the coast of Spain, but it was in sight, and it wasn't dark. Overhead the sky rippled with green light that belonged at the poles. While he knew it was caused by the solar flare activity, it was unnerving. Anxiety twisted in his gut. He had nothing to worry about. The crew wasn't worried and if there was any danger, they'd have headed in already.

"So where's this whale?" Oliver scanned the ocean, searching for the whale. It was dark except for the areas that were reflecting the eerie green light. Earlier there'd been dozens of boats on the water. There'd even been a few cruise ships in the distance. He thought he could still see one lit up so the guests could party.

"It should be around here," Jack said. "Another vessel reported it. We often give each other tips if we see something interesting." He smiled.

Tahlia scampered up the stairs to join them. Her hair was wet, and she didn't seem pissed at all. Henry, on the other hand, was his usual scowling self. He'd wanted this damn trip, had begged Dad to pay for it, and now he was hating every minute.

Oliver almost felt sorry for him. Nothing made Henry happy.

"Have you seen it yet?" Tahlia leaned on the railing and peered down like the whale was going to stick its fin up and wave at them.

The boat headed toward a patch of water that seemed to have movement. A warm breeze skated over Oliver's skin. "Is that it?"

"I don't know," Jack said.

They were all leaning on the railing now.

The creature breached the surface only a few meters away and blew out a stream of air and water. Oliver laughed, letting go of the tension. They'd seen the whale, and it had seen them. They could head back to port.

"Look, there's a second one," Tahlia said, pointing at a second large shape.

Oliver followed to where she was pointing. A V had formed in the water as it moved swiftly toward them. Its body broke the surface…where was its fin?

Jack frowned. "I don't think that's a—"

The second animal crashed into the whale. Blood bloomed in the water and spread fast.

"What the hell?" Oliver stepped back, then decided that he'd rather be holding the railing.

"Get us out of here, Paul!" Jack shouted. "There's something attacking the whale."

An overly large wave slopped bloody water over the deck and the boat lurched at a horrible angle, as though something was trying to tip them off. Oliver dropped his beer and gripped the railing with both hands. Tahlia screamed.

"What was that?"

"A killer whale or a shark," Jack said, but he didn't sound very convinced.

Sharks had dorsal fins, and so did killer whales.

"Why aren't we moving?" Henry asked, his knuckles white around the rail.

Oliver looked up from the water where the whale had been attacked. There was no sign of it now, or the other creature.

Where there had been open water, there was now a dark coastline. Maybe they'd gotten turned around. But when he glanced over his shoulder, he couldn't see the bright coast of Spain either.

CHAPTER 2

Jack stared out at the water. Waves slapped the side of the yacht, washing away the whale blood. The twin hulls made it a very stable craft, but he wished they were in a powered motorboat and could put on a burst of speed to get back to where they should be. His gut churned. He really wanted to join the guests in freaking out, but he couldn't, so he swallowed his fear.

The world had suddenly gone dark. Like someone had flipped a switch and turned off the whole of Spain. There were no other boats on the water, either.

"I'm going to find out what the problem is." Because them not moving was only a part of the problem. How had everything gone dark?

He glanced up at the green, rippling sky. Another time he might have found it beautiful, tonight it was eerie and for a few heartbeats it felt like they were the only humans alive. He shook off the feeling, knowing he was being melodramatic.

There must have been a large solar flare, and it had knocked out the power grid or something. He was sure there'd been warnings about disturbances—but he'd thought they meant minor, not taking out an entire country. A whole coastline.

He moved quickly and carefully over the bloody deck, trying not to think about the whale he'd seen be attacked. Of course whales were attacked. Sharks ate them, and there were always sharks in the water, even if he didn't see them. But it hadn't looked much like a shark. But then, not every shark was the same. Perhaps it had been one of those rare and ugly kinds. But he couldn't convince himself of that because it hadn't looked like even an ugly shark.

He leaned into the bridge. "Paul, why aren't we moving?"

"Everything malfunctioned, and the screens shut down. So I cut the engine. Now I've got no radio, no navigation and the depth sounder is telling me that the Mediterranean is much deeper than it should be."

Jack nodded. Everything was messed up, so stopping was a good idea. "But we do still have engines?"

The last thing he wanted was to be stranded in the dark with no way of radioing for help.

"Yeah. But without navigation, where am I going?"

"North…We know Spain is that way." And if not Spain, then France. Though he wasn't sure which way was north without the familiar lights. "And if we accidentally head south, we'll hit the coast of Africa."

Paul worked his jaw and shook his head. "I'm not going anywhere until some emergency lights come on. Look out the window, kid. Not even the lighthouses are working, and I can't see the cruise ship, can you?"

Jack bristled. He hated being called kid, but he did as he was told. There was nothing out there as far as he could see. The aurora was still lighting up the sky, casting its unearthly light. Damn solar flare. "We were within sight of the coast. The freak wave wasn't that big. It couldn't have washed us that far off course."

The wave had barely rocked the boat. Like the others, he'd been watching the whale, but he'd also been watching the guests. The last thing he wanted was to lose one overboard, especially when the whale was being attacked.

"The only coast is that one." Paul pointed in the other direction.

Jack saw the silhouette of trees in the distance. There shouldn't be any trees there. That should've been open water heading for North Africa. He checked the rest of the windows, searching for a familiar landmark. He'd done the cruise along the coast at least twenty times, but everything was alien in the unnatural dark. "What are you suggesting?"

"We send up a flare and wait." He gave Jack a pointed glare.

Jack rested his head against the door frame. There should be emergency lights flicking on by now. The lighthouses should be on. "Try the radio again."

Paul handed it to him. It was dead, not even static.

"Is the battery flat, is our battery flat?"

"We seem to be fine, for the moment."

"What does that mean?"

"I've been sailing here for over a decade. I know this coast, this sea. I've been in storms and becalmed when using sails. And I don't recognize a damn thing out there. The skyline is wrong."

"Maybe the aurora is making everything seem strange." Jack pushed down on the panic that wanted to break free. Paul was right. There were trees where there should be none, and while he couldn't see lights on the coasts, the shape in the distance was also wrong.

"It was a freak wave. We're still in the Mediterranean."

Paul stared out the window. "I know we should be, but what I'm seeing isn't the Mediterranean. Maybe the solar flare created some kind of new Bermuda Triangle."

That wasn't comforting.

"So where are we?"

"No idea."

Jack stared out the window at the trees in the distance. The last slip of sun was about to be swallowed by the water, but that at least gave him a direction. And the trees were in the south, the wrong way if they wanted to return to Spain. The whale, or the thing that had attacked it, broke the surface. It was too far away for him to be able to tell what it was, only that it was big.

"Paul, did you see what attacked the whale?"

"No, but a shark attack is not the experience we want to provide."

Jack didn't care about the damn guest experience right now. "I don't think it was a shark."

"Killer whale, whatever. We're fine on the boat, so we wait it out. Come daylight, we'll have radio back and we can call for help. Even if we don't, people will search for us."

Jack didn't want to be on the ocean all night. Not with those enormous creatures swimming around. "Maybe we should move closer to the shore."

Even if it was the wrong one.

"I'm not sailing blindly through the night over unfamiliar water. If we hit rocks, we will be stuffed."

"We don't have satellites?"

"Nothing. The solar flare seems to have taken out everything."

The ocean glimmered green under the aurora, and Jack was sure he saw a few more creatures break the surface, but it might have been his imagination making up sea monsters. No emergency lights came on. With no lighthouses to warn them of rocks and no satellites, they had no idea where they were going. It might be best to stay put.

Shouting on the deck made them both look up.

"Shit, you left them unattended," Paul snapped.

And in that time Henry had got a ski free. He was pulling a life vest and arguing with his girlfriend. Jack didn't waste any time; he ran.

He reached for the skis. "What are you doing?"

"I'm not sitting here, waiting for rescue. The coast is right there." Henry pointed at the trees. "I'll be drinking in the bar in under ten minutes."

"You don't know where you're going. That's not Spain." Jack pointed at the trees.

"France, Morocco, wherever. You can get me in the morning."

"We don't have any navigation equipment. While we figure out what to do, it's best to stay on the boat."

Henry did up his life jacket. "Come on, Tahlia."

Tahlia glanced between Jack and Henry. "I don't know. We can party on the boat."

Jack muttered a curse. "Please stay on the boat." As he went past to argue some more with Paul—and risk his job—he grabbed Oliver's arm. "Keep your brother on the boat."

"What's going on? Henry thinks we were hit by a solar flare." Oliver nodded his head toward the illuminated sky.

"Yeah, probably. The whole coast is dark, so it was a big one."

The jet ski engine revved.

"Go." Jack gave Oliver a push, then took off toward the bridge to convince Paul to take them in a little way. The depth sounder was fine.

Paul stared at him. "Make yourself useful and send a flare through while I secure the boat for the night."

"Take us in. That's all Henry wants. It might be safer for all of us." How many of those big things were out there? If they were sharks—and they had to be—would they attack a boat?

The jet ski with two people on board shot past the window on their way to the coast.

"Fuck." Paul slammed his hand onto the edge of the control panel.

"Go after them. You can't leave them out there on that." Jack's heart bounced high in his throat.

"We don't know where we are. I have no navigation. If I drive around, we are going to become more lost."

"Just go for the damn coast."

"I'm not risking the ship."

Jack's heart beat hard, thumping against his ribs. "Please, can we collect them?"

Henry and Tahlia were nothing more than a shadow gliding over the water.

"They're going to make it, and they can raise the alarm," Paul said with a smug smile.

Jack glanced at Paul. "Assuming there's people there, right? You don't know where we are."

Paul opened his mouth to argue, but his mouth kept stretching open. Jack lifted his gaze to the window, dread already swelling in his stomach. Something else had spotted the ski. The creature arrowed through the water after Henry and Tahlia.

"Do something!"

"What?"

"Fucking drive the boat." Jack shoved Paul away from the controls. He started the boat and turned it, keeping his gaze firmly on Henry. They weren't going to make it. The creature was faster. He knew it, but he had to try.

Paul punched him in the side of the head. "Don't be a fool. Look at the size of that thing."

Jack looked. He watched as it rose out of the water and latched its jaws around the jet ski and passengers and dragged them under. It took several seconds for the waves to calm to ripples. He searched the surface, hoping that one of them had jumped clear.

Nothing.
Then something scraped the bottom of the ship.

CHAPTER 3

Oliver watched as his brother got the jet ski in the water. "Don't be an idiot. We don't know what's out there."

He wasn't sure what had attacked the whale, but he was damn sure it hadn't been a shark. It had been almost the same size as the whale for a start.

"We were out on the sea all day, and now it's dark you're scared?" Henry laughed. "I'm not sitting here all night."

"We'll move soon, I'm sure." Oliver would much rather be on land, but he wasn't going to cross the sea on a jet ski to get there.

Henry turned to Tahlia. "Let's go, get your life vest on."

She worried at her lower lip and glanced at the bridge where Paul and Jack were talking. While they talked, the boat bobbed in the green lit water. He wished he'd read more about the damage the solar flares and magnetic drift could do instead of laughing it off like everyone else. Scientists were always putting forward the worst-case scenario. Oliver doubted it was because they were trying to scare anyone, more like they were trying to make people listen and prepare.

"What makes you so sure that's Spain?" Olvier pressed, trying to stall his brother. "And if everything is dead, what's the rush?"

Henry grinned at him. "I want to know what's going on. I'll send help for the rest of you…in the morning."

Tahlia found her voice. "I saw the thing that attacked the whale. What if it's still out there?"

"Babe, it won't be interested in us, not when there's whales to eat. Plus, it will be afraid of the motor. You want to wait here with them? They're too scared to do anything but wait for rescue." Henry gestured at the bridge.

He had a point. They should do something. But what was there to do when the world, or at least their part of it, had gone dark. Circuits fried by the solar flares. Where were the emergency lights? Shouldn't there be some?

And the other ships. There'd been a cruise ship within sight that couldn't have gone dark too, could it?

"Just wait a bit, Henry. It won't be long until some lights come on."

Henry revved the ski and pulled away from the boat.

"Get back here. It's not safe."

He watched his brother's progress, hope lifting his heart with each passing second. They were going to make it to shore.

The boat's engine hummed to life, loud in the night. Good, they were going after Henry and heading for the shore.

Something lurched out of the water, and before Oliver opened his mouth, the creature had taken Henry and Tahlia in its jaws.

"No!" But they were already gone.

"Oh my god," Noah said, moving up beside him. "I can't believe they left the ship."

Oliver couldn't move. He kept waiting for them to bob to the surface in their bright orange life vests. This couldn't be real.

The yacht shuddered and rocked as something nudged it from below. Oliver stepped back from the edge, but there was nothing to hold on to but the railing. The fiberglass hulls no longer seemed quite so sturdy.

Noah swore. "I think we should go inside."

But his brother was in the water. "Henry…" The empty water gleamed, taunting them. "We need to get over there. What if they're injured?"

"I don't think…"

Oliver ignored him. He made his way up to the bridge, ignoring the rocking. Jack held the side of his head. Paul was at the controls, turning off the engine. "What are you doing? Get over there and look for my brother."

"We're going to wait here for help. Jack's going to fire off a couple of flares to let people know where we are."

"Like hell. We have to search the water for Henry." He didn't like his brother most of the time, but Henry was still his brother. Henry never took no for an answer, and few people ever dared to challenge him. And now he was gone. If he'd waited… he could have been the one standing here demanding that Paul take the boat in as planned.

"We have a limited amount of fuel, and I don't know if our battery was damaged. So we need to be very conservative," Paul said.

The boat was nudged again, making them all reach for something to hold on to; not that it would matter if they were tipped into the ocean.

Jack glowered at Paul. "Whatever is bumping us, isn't going to get bored."

"It might. We should stay where we are," Paul said firmly.

"You need to find Henry," Oliver shouted. "And if we head for the coast, then the creature beneath us might piss off."

"He's right, Paul. We have to look for Henry. And we can't stay here."

"There's nothing out there." Paul pointed at the water where Henry and Tahlia and the ski had been.

Paul was right. There was nothing but more water. No boats, no whales, nothing familiar at all. Oliver didn't want to admit that Henry was gone. They'd hated each other growing up, always jostling to be the favourite. They'd been trying to be friends since Oliver had started college. "Please can we head for the coast and look for my brother."

"No. I don't want to end up in some random place," Paul said. "With no navigation equipment we could run into trouble."

"We're in trouble," Oliver snapped. "And since I'm the paying guest, I say we search for Henry and head for shore."

"Uh, guys…" Emma, the cook, stuck her head into the now crowded bridge. "I suggest we move the argument along to the conclusion. It's dark and something is interested in the boat. I'd rather be on land for the night."

"I'd rather be home." Oliver crossed his arms and fixed Paul with what he hoped was something close to Henry's glare. "Drive."

Paul's jaw worked like he was chewing through a boot. "Fine. I suggest you and Jack go and fire up a couple of flares. Maybe we'll be rescued before dinner."

The boat jolted again.

Or maybe they'd be the ones getting eaten.

CHAPTER 4

Jack grabbed the flare gun, though he wasn't sure it would be much use. If nothing was familiar, then where the hell were they?

Oliver followed him out of the bridge. "You can drive the boat, right?"

"Sure." He could, but he wasn't licenced. And he wasn't sure he wanted to. "Let's just fire the flares and see what happens."

Overhead, the sky had lost its green gleam, but there were still no lights on the coast, or the water—aside from their boat. Paul wasn't rushing their journey to the strange coast. As much as Jack would like him to hurry, the cautious approach was the right one. Wrecking the boat would only cause them more problems.

"What if nothing happens?"

"What do you mean?" Jack loaded the gun.

"What if there's no one out there?"

"There has to be." But when he cast his gaze over the water, he wasn't so sure. "Did you see what…what took Henry?" He finished.

Oliver nodded and kept his gaze on the deck.

Shit, he could've handled that better. "How are you holding up?" That sounded pathetic once it had left his lips. What was the right thing to say after watching two guests, Oliver's brother and girlfriend, be taken by some kind of sea monster?

"How do you think?"

"I'm sorry." Aside from physically restraining Henry, what else had he been supposed to do?

"I think it was the same thing that attacked the whale. And I don't think it was a shark."

"Neither do I. I don't know what it was." Which scared him more than he liked to admit.

The boat groaned and tilted as something started investigating again. The water was now too dark to see anything. While Jack had spent a lot of time on boats as a kid and working on them as an adult, he'd never been afraid about what might be in the water until now. He'd always been confident that he knew what he was doing.

Now he had no idea.

He hoped that come daylight, everything would make sense. They wouldn't be lost, and they'd be able to laugh about what had happened.

Well, everyone but Henry and Tahlia. Shit. There were going to be all kinds of problems when they got back after this job. He was pretty sure he wouldn't have a job.

The creature surfaced next to the boat. Its head was the size of a car, and its teeth were as long as Jack's hand. He was sure it was looking at them. Then its body rolled through the water, in what seemed like a never-ending movement before its tail finally flicked up and it vanished.

Jack stared at where it had just been. That wasn't any kind of sea creature he knew of.

"That was a mosasaur," Oliver whispered. "That's not possible."

"A what?" He couldn't have heard right, because it sounded like Oliver was naming a dinosaur.

"It looked like a mosasaur." Oliver glanced at him. "A dinosaur."

"No, it had to be a shark or something."

"There was no dorsal fin."

Jack had noticed that, too. And the flippers were the wrong shape. Everything about it was the wrong shape. "It can't be a mosasaur, they died out millions of years ago."

If it was a mosasaur, what did that mean?

He lifted the flare gun.

Oliver put his hand on Jack's arm. "And if it attracts more dinosaurs?"

"Well, they'll be drawn away from the boat, won't they?" Jack gave him a grim smile. This wasn't something that he'd been briefed on how to deal with. There was no company policy on being lost and seeing a dinosaur—if it was a dinosaur. "How did you know it was a dinosaur?"

Oliver shrugged. "Usual obsession as a kid."

"Are you sure that's what it was?"

"You got a better suggestion?"

Jack shook his head. "It doesn't seem quite real, does it?"

"I wish it wasn't. I want Henry to come out of his cabin and demand to know why dinner is late." Oliver scrubbed a hand over his face.

"Hurry up," Paul shouted.

Jack lifted the flare gun and fired it into the sky. He watched it arc up before exploding. The night lit up, and when the flare was gone, it was darker than ever. Even the stars seemed strange.

Around the boat the water rippled in the starlight. Any other time he'd have found the sight pretty.

"What now?" Oliver asked.

"Now we wait."

"Isn't there anything else you can do? Don't you have an emergency beacon or something you can activate?"

Jack pressed his lips together. They did. But would Paul want to activate it? And if Europe had gone dark because of the solar flarc, they were going to be really low down on the priority list. "I'll ask Paul."

The boat rocked, and they both grabbed the railing. Going overboard would mean death.

Oliver's eyes widened. "Do you think the mosasaur will attack the boat?"

"It's never seen a boat…it's probably trying to figure out if it's edible." The boat wasn't, but they were. What if the mosasaur could smell them or hear their heartbeats?

If he could smell Emma's cooking, could the dinosaur?

The boat tipped again as it was nudged. How many were down there? Was it one or was the sea teaming with dinosaurs? He closed his eyes, his stomach knotted so tight he didn't think he could breathe.

Even if there were only a few big ones, like there were only a few whales, there were still plenty of other smaller things. There had to be for the big things to eat, and right now, even the small things were dangerous. It would only take one overly inquisitive dino to tip the boat over.

The dark shore became clearer as Paul puttered the boat closer. He'd been hoping for a beach or a fishing village, but there was nothing but a tangle of trees.

Paul slowed the boat, then killed the engine. They couldn't risk damaging the hull on unseen roots or trees or rocks. This wasn't a shore; this was a mangrove swamp. "Tie her up, not too tight."

"Will do." Mangrove swamps were tidal. He didn't know if it was high or low tide at the moment. And he didn't know what would be worse. What he knew about mangrove shorelines wasn't good. Had snakes been invented yet? What about crocodiles? Even if they didn't exist, he was sure there were plenty of other nasties lurking.

"This doesn't look good," Oliver whispered, like he was worried about waking something up.

From the sounds of the night, there were plenty of things awake. There were whistles and growls and gulps and other sounds he'd never heard an animal make. Jack's skin broke out in gooseflesh, and he suppressed a shudder.

"No, it doesn't." A large insect buzzed past his head. "I think we should go in. Emma's made dinner and we can't let our rations go to waste."

"What do you mean?"

"I mean we have limited food and water on board." And fuel.

At some point soon they were going to have to do some hard math. Where were they going to get fresh water from, and was there anything here they could hunt and eat, or would it all kill them?

"Someone will have seen the flare. They'll be coming to get us soon." Jack forced a smile and clapped the younger man on the shoulder.

"Yeah. I'm sure they will," Oliver said, but he sounded even less convinced than Jack.

They went down to the mess. Jack should eat in the galley with Emma, but she was sitting at the table with Noah. She glanced up at him, her eyebrows pinched and her face pale. They'd been working together for six months and dating for four of them. No one knew, though. He sure as hell didn't want Paul to find out.

Paul stomped below and sat.

There was no division between crew and guests anymore. They were all stranded, and everyone needed to be working together.

Oliver sat down next to Noah and squeezed his hand.

Jack wasn't the only one moving through the boat at night to meet his lover. He sat and stared at the meal Emma had made. It was growing cold, but no one was touching the fish.

No one spoke.

The boat rocked gently, but every bump on the hull made him flinch. His heartbeat was too fast and too loud.

"We should eat," Emma said.

Oliver nodded. "How much food is left?"

She stared at him. "Enough."

"Enough for how long?" Noah pressed.

"We'll be rescued before we need to worry about that." Paul helped himself to a piece of fish and loaded salad onto his plate like nothing was amiss. "Jack sent up a flare."

Jack's face was hot from the punch. If Paul had turned for shore instead of trying to provide a five-star experience so he could scrounge an extra tip from the whale sighting, they wouldn't be in this mess.

Paul started eating before anyone else had taken anything.

Oliver glanced at Jack. And Jack knew what he was going to say before he opened his mouth. "The creature that attacked the whale was a mosasaur."

Saying it out loud, to everyone, didn't make the monster any more real. It seemed absurd to be talking about dinosaurs.

"What are you talking about? Sea monsters?" Paul scoffed.

"It's a kind of dinosaur," Oliver said, not put off by Paul's disbelief.

Noah frowned. "How can that be?"

"It can't be," Paul said before shovelling in a mouthful of food.

What Jack knew about dinosaurs could be written on the back of his hand in reasonably large letters. There were meat eaters and plant eaters. They were big, and he much preferred a few million years between him and them. He put some food on his plate, hoping to encourage the others to eat.

Noah glanced around the table. "Tahlia and Henry, were they eaten by the same thing?"

Oliver closed his eyes and spoke through gritted teeth. "Yes. I have no idea how I'm going to explain what happened to Mum." His voice broke. "She'll blame me."

"No, she won't." Jack said. She'd blame him and Paul and the charter company. They were going to get royally fucked over.

Paul's face whitened, as if he'd reached the same conclusion. *Yeah, that's right, Captain. That's on you.*

Jack turned his attention to the food, but he didn't taste a single bite. There was a dinosaur out there that had already tasted human flesh.

Gradually the others started eating, and for the first night of this cruise it was a silent meal. There was no laughter—though usually that had been Henry's, as he'd made fun of Oliver.

"We need to make a plan," Jack said when he finished.

"We'll be rescued tomorrow." Paul smiled. "By the time we're sitting on deck, sipping coffee, a rescue vessel will be pulling alongside."

"If the power is out and communication lines are down, I don't think they're going to be in a rush to get us," Jack said.

"Have you activated the distress beacon?" Emma asked. She was picking at her meal, but not actually eating.

Paul shook his head. "No. Because we aren't in distress. We aren't sinking, and no one is injured."

Oliver stared at him. "My brother is dead, and you don't know where we are. Don't you think you should activate it so it's easier for the rescue boat to pull up alongside?" He mimicked Paul's words, but it was clear he didn't believe what Paul had said.

Paul's features tightened before he forced a smile. "If it helps you sleep better, I'll turn it on before we go to bed."

Who the hell was going to be sleeping tonight? Jack felt like he'd drunk ten cups of coffee. Even his skin was jittery.

The boat shuddered as something brushed against the hull. Five humans, neatly packed into one fiberglass lunchbox.

Would they even survive the night?

CHAPTER 5

Jack stood in the galley, washing the dishes while Emma dried. The food that hadn't been eaten she'd put in the fridge, not wanting to waste anything. Though for how long the fridge would be running, Jack didn't know. "Do you think we'll be all right? Will they actually be looking for us?"

"We missed check in, so they'll realize something is up." And a fisher or another boat would see the whale carcass, or maybe even find the mosasaur that attacked the whale. Or would they think it had eaten them too? "They might already be looking for us."

Though they would be looking in the wrong place. This was not the Mediterranean. This wasn't part of Spain or even the coast of North Africa. While he didn't know as much as Paul, if Paul didn't know where they were, they were lost.

She stared at him.

And he buckled. "I think we're screwed. I don't think anyone will find us. We don't even know where here is." The words tumbled out. "There are dinosaurs in the water…" he drew in a breath and looked up at the ceiling. "How is that even possible? It shouldn't be."

"Wait… you don't know where we are? Like at all?"

He shook his head. "Paul has no idea, either. We have no navigation and no familiar landmarks."

"But you must have some idea. Where do you think we are?"

He swallowed hard, not wanting to say what he thought out loud.

"Jack?"

"It's stupid."

"We're docked in a mangrove swamp that shouldn't be there, and a dinosaur ate two of the guests. I don't think anything is stupid at the moment."

He nodded. "What if the solar flare activity sent us back in time?"

She didn't laugh. "How?"

"Wrong place at the wrong time? The mosasaur appeared and attacked the whale and then we became lost."

"If we are in the past, then it's going to make it hard for people to find us. So I hope you're wrong."

"So do I, because if I'm right, there'll be more dinosaurs."

Her eyes widened. Jack put his arm around her. "Come morning, everything will look different. I'm sure it was only the aurora making everything seem weird. It probably wasn't even a mosasaur. Oliver is scared and seeing monsters."

She leaned into him. "I don't want to be here."

"Neither do I."

"Does Paul have a plan?"

"He wanted to wait at sea." They should be out there with their emergency beacon on, waiting for rescue. "He's already punched me once for disagreeing, but at least we came in for the night."

"What will we do in the morning?"

Jack closed his eyes and rested his cheek on her head. "I don't know. Hopefully wake up, find everything back online, and head into the nearest Spanish port."

"And if it's not?"

"Figure something out." He released her and stepped back, ready to finish washing the dishes. "How much fresh water do we have?"

"If no one showers, enough for two weeks." She stilled with the plate to be dried in her hand. "You don't really think…"

"I think we need to prepare for the worst." Which meant they'd gone back to a time where dinosaurs lived. But even if they were lost in some weird part of the Mediterranean, they still had to make it to a port and if Europe had been hit by a solar flare, things were going to be hard.

"Right…what's worse than being stalked by a mosasaur?"

"Being stalked by two?" It was a bad joke, and Emma didn't laugh. "We have food and water and a place to sleep. We'll be okay." For tonight. Tomorrow…he desperately wanted Paul to be right and that they would be rescued. "Come on, let's finish this and go and…"

There was no TV to watch. While they had laptops, there was no point in trying to send email or chat to friends or family as there was no internet.

"We should sleep," she finished for him.

"Yeah." That was all there was left to do. She wouldn't be able to text him to come and visit during the night. "Did you want company?"

She worried at her lower lip and turned away to stow the plate.

"Am I interrupting?" Paul asked.

"Just finishing up. You might want to tell the guests not to shower. We need to save water," Jack said.

Paul laughed. "Stop worrying."

Jack scowled at him.

Emma smiled and stepped forward. "I like the way you think positively, but it might take them more than a day to figure out what's going on and find us. Did you turn on the beacon?"

"Yeah."

Jack would check that he had because he didn't trust Paul.

Paul turned to him. "I don't want you worrying the guests."

"They're already worried. Two of them are dead," Jack snapped.

Paul stepped up and put his finger on Jack's chest. "That's your fault for not stopping them. I'll make sure that's in my report. I'm not wearing that responsibility."

Jack pushed Paul's hand away. "You're in charge. Every decision that is made comes down to you. You had the chance to take us to shore straight away, but you freaked out because your instruments went dead."

"Enough." Emma stepped between them. "We're here now and stuck until someone comes to get us or we figure out where we are and head home."

Going home meant sailing over open water with God knew what swimming around them. At that moment, he didn't feel brave enough to do that. He hoped that come dawn everything would make sense. "How much fuel do we have left?"

Paul shrugged. "It doesn't matter."

"It *does* matter. If we don't know, we can't make plans. We don't know how far we can travel," Jack pressed.

"Rescue will come, and we'll be fine."

Emma frowned. "What about the mosasaur?"

"You don't actually believe that, do you?" Paul scoffed. "A dinosaur? Really?"

Jack crossed his arms; he believed it was a dinosaur that took Henry and Tahlia. "It sure as hell wasn't a shark."

He glanced at Emma, expecting her to spill that he thought they'd somehow been transported to the past, but her lips were pressed tightly together.

"Then we're safe here, aren't we?" Paul gave them both a filthy look and spun on his heel and stalked away.

***

Inside his cabin, it was easy for Oliver to pretend that everything was as it should be. He could close his eyes, put on some music and forget. Oliver wished that he'd told Henry that he wasn't coming on this trip, and that their father had cancelled the trip. Except that wouldn't have happened. Henry would've dragged along some of his other friends to make up the numbers. And this still would've happened. Except Oliver would have been safe at home.

His thoughts spiralled downward.

He was going to die here, wherever here was. He didn't know where the dinosaurs had come from. What if he died here?

What would his mother do if both her children were dead?

His father would demand answers. He'd expect someone to pay for the loss. But that wasn't the same as being missed.

While he knew some people would miss him, the world would move on. Without Henry—that would piss Henry off, as he liked to think that he was the centre of everything. And if he wasn't, he made himself. He smiled and charmed his way into everything—until things didn't go his way. Then his temper came out.

Oliver would never bear witness to another one of his brother's cringe inducing tirades. At the moment, he'd happily withstand it just to have him back. To be back on land and not lost.

The family name.

The family money.

None of it mattered if he couldn't get home.

He squeezed his eyes closed.

Someone tried the handle of his cabin. He'd locked it, something he hadn't done previously when alone. The person then knocked.

Oliver didn't move. He wasn't in the mood for company. He lay still, listening for when whoever it was walked away. Let them think him asleep. Maybe if he slept, when he woke up, all of this would just be a nightmare.

The boat rocked, and it sounded like someone was moving around on the deck. He frowned. More than one person. What if it wasn't people but more dinosaurs?

No, it was probably Emma, Jack, and Paul doing something. But the longer he listened, the less like people it sounded. He was sure something growled, then there were the whistles and chirps. It was like doing one of those zoo night tours, except the animals weren't locked up.

What if the animals came downstairs?

The door to his cabin suddenly seemed too flimsy. What weapons did he have?

He partially sat up and glanced around his dark room, lit only by starlight sliding through the porthole. There was nothing besides his laptop. He was about to reach out and grab it when something scrabbled against the hull on the other side of the fiberglass wall.

Oliver shuddered. He hadn't closed the curtain on the porthole because he hadn't wanted to be in complete darkness. Now he was too scared to get up and do it. His muscles locked him in place. He couldn't even roll his eyes to look in case something was peering in and watching him.

Better to not move.

He softened his breathing until he wasn't sure he was breathing at all.

CHAPTER 6

With the boat tied up for the night, Jack and Emma sat up in bed, drinking coffee and playing cards. They'd tried going to bed, but neither of them had been able to sleep, so they'd given up. They'd grabbed a map and spent time guessing where they could be, but they couldn't have been swept far off course and nothing explained the mosasaurs.

He'd almost convinced himself that it must have been a weird kind of shark, and that Paul was right, and Oliver was overwrought and imagining things. But Oliver didn't seem like that kind of guy. He was quiet and calm, and clearly dating his friend—he'd seen Noah slinking between cabins on the first night—and he knew too well the feeling of needing to keep things a secret. He couldn't remember the last time he'd been open about who he was dating.

It had become a habit.

Something landed on the deck above. They both froze.

Jack glanced at Emma as he listened.

The scrabble and thump were quickly followed by several more. He wished they were being boarded by human pirates. That he could have dealt with. It was a threat that he could understand. Hell, he could even ask the pirates where they were, and to be honest, getting ransomed for money almost seemed like a good idea.

"Monkeys?" Emma whispered a little too hopefully. They'd both decided that they must be somewhere on the coast of Africa, even though that was just as improbable as dinosaurs in the water.

The growling and the hissing didn't sound like monkeys.

He allowed himself a grim smile at the idea of dinosaurs dressed up as pirates. Except they didn't need a cutlass or pistols. They had claws and teeth.

"Is all the food locked away?" That's what animals wanted. He tried not to think about the fact that they could be considered food.

Emma nodded. "Everything is in cupboards or the fridge."

Like a few delicate doors would stop animals from taking whatever they wanted. "Do you think Paul locked the bridge?"

"I don't think we're going to be hijacked."

"I was more worried about them destroying the controls."

She glanced up as something clattered across the deck. "Do you want to check?"

"Not really." But if he didn't, and the controls were damaged, they were well and truly stranded. Unlike Paul, he wasn't confident in being found.

Jack got off the bed, the boat tilted, and something fell into the water. He hoped it was one of the animals—and not something vital, like life rafts.

His body pulsed as adrenaline flooded his veins. "I'm going to speak to Paul."

"You're not his favourite person."

"He likes me well enough when I follow orders." It was only when Jack questioned him that there were problems. He didn't want to work with Paul again…he released a shaky breath. That wouldn't be a problem. He wouldn't be working in this industry ever again. Letting two passengers die wasn't a great thing to have on his record.

"I'll go with you."

"Maybe you should wait in the cabin." Would it be safer? The doors were made for privacy, not protection.

"I don't want you out there alone with those things." She finished her cold cup of coffee. "Let's grab some knives from the kitchen."

"You planning on killing and cooking one up?" He forced a smile.

She gave a small shrug. "Depends on what it is and how long we're here for."

"Hopefully not that long."

"Agreed."

"Okay, so we check in with Paul first, then we get knives from the kitchen." Then they'd have to go up to the bridge and lock it. He really wanted to know what was making those weird noises. The not knowing was making his hair stand on end and his gut knot.

Emma slid off the bed and gathered up the blanket. "That's as good a plan as any."

And better than anything Paul had come up with.

"What are you doing?"

"If one comes at us, we can throw the blanket over it. It won't kill it, but it will slow it down enough for us to run away."

He kissed the end of her nose. "I like the way you think."

"Good. Let's do this."

Yeah, before he lost his nerve. He opened the cabin door a crack and peered along the dark corridor. The boat wasn't that big, and the corridor wasn't very long, but even in the dark it appeared to be free of movement. Paul's cabin was at the end, and it was the biggest of the three crew cabins.

As quietly as he could, Jack edged down the corridor. The worst bit would be knocking on the door. He glanced over his shoulder. Emma followed, guarding his back with the blanket. He should be guarding hers.

"Hurry up," she hissed.

He knocked. The deck went silent. Coincidence, or had they heard him? Sweat trickled down his back.

The door opened. Paul had his shirt off and a bottle of red wine in his other hand. He was choosing now to get drunk?

"What do you want?"

"Did you take wine, meant for the guests, from my galley?" Emma asked.

Jack stared at him. That must have been why Paul had come into the galley while he and Emma had been doing dishes. No doubt he'd snuck back after they'd gone to bed.

"And? After today I figured I needed a drink." Paul took a sip from the bottle as if to prove the point.

The thumping and scrabbling overhead resumed.

"We aren't supposed to drink on the job." That was one rule Jack always followed. He'd thought Paul did, too. Maybe today was the exception and Paul had the right idea. Drink, and forget tonight, and deal with their new reality tomorrow.

Paul went to close the door, and Jack shoved his foot in the way. "Did you close the bridge?"

"I don't know."

They didn't usually bother unless they were pulled into port. Did this count as a port?

"Yes or no, Paul?" Emma asked. "If it's open and whatever is up there damages the controls, we're screwed."

"Rescue will come. You just want to take over," Paul sneered.

"I can't fuck up any worse than you." Jack regretted the words as soon as they were out of his mouth, even though they were true. "If we'd followed the plan and gone in for the night instead of going after the whale sighting—"

"It's about the guests—"

"And two of them are dead." Jack clenched his teeth so he couldn't say anything else. He forced out a slow breath. "Someone needs to lock the bridge, Captain."

"I've been drinking. It would be dangerous for me to be on deck. And since you're the one who wants to be a hero, you'd best go up there." Paul shoved the door hard against Jack's foot.

Jack yanked his foot back and stood there staring at the wood veneer for several heartbeats. "Fuck."

Claws danced over the deck, and snarls filled the night. It sounded worse than the bachelor party he'd once worked on a much bigger charter boat.

"Shoo," Emma said, flapping the blanket.

Jack turned. Something small moved in the shadowy corridor. It was about knee high, and it might have been a monkey, given that it had a tail, but it also had spiky feathers and pranced like an oversized chicken as it watched them.

He knew what it was, but he didn't want to believe it.

"That's a dinosaur," he whispered.

"Yeah. Or some kind of weird beakless bird."

Jack nodded. He was no dinosaur expert—though he knew a stegosaurus from a T-Rex—but it didn't look like a plant eater. He didn't want to discover what its actual dietary requirements were.

Emma stepped forward and flapped more aggressively. The dinosaur shrank back like it feared them, filling Jack with more confidence. They could do this.

"They are small and noisy. It will be like running through a flock of oversized seagulls." A toothy flock of seagulls.

Come daylight, they could assess the damage to the boat and figure out how to get home. Fast. Before more dinosaurs found them.

CHAPTER 7

Together, Jack and Emma moved quickly and quietly through the crew sleeping quarters. The dinosaur ran in front of them, its claws clicking over the wooden flooring.

Yeah, that's right, dino, run.

Emma kept flapping the blanket. Maybe it was the blanket it was scared of, not the humans. Either way, it didn't matter as they made it to the kitchen.

Emma didn't turn on a light. She knew where everything was even in the moonlit galley. She handed him a knife. "Be careful, it's very sharp."

What was he supposed to do with it? He couldn't put it in his pocket. "What else do you have that could be weaponized? Meat mallet? Rolling pin?"

"This is a galley, not a commercial kitchen." She huffed out a breath, then opened a different drawer. "Meat cleaver?"

It looked like a small axe. "What do you use that for?"

"Cutting the heads off fish usually."

Jack happily took it from her and handed back the knife. She kept the knife, clearly unbothered about cutting herself with it, but then she used it all the time. She gave him a nod, and they turned to leave the galley. Three of the small dinosaurs watched them from the mess.

One perched on the table in the spill of moonlight. The spiky feathers stuck out of its arms and down its back in tufts of orange.

"They do have feathers," Emma whispered. "It looks like they're half plucked already."

He grinned, even though there were now three of them below deck. "When come back below, we need to shut the hatch."

He didn't want to do it on the way up, in case they needed to make a hasty escape.

"Agreed, let's keep moving before they decide we aren't a threat, and that we might be tasty."

That wasn't a thought he needed. "Let's hope it's more of the same up there."

He took the blanket from her, tossed it over his shoulder and went up the stairs first, hoping that whatever was up there was small enough that the blanket would confuse and immobilize it.

"Should we make noise and pretend to be scary?" Emma hissed just before he stuck his head out to have a look.

He paused and glanced at her. "What? They've never seen humans before. They don't know that we aren't really superior predators."

"True. But all we need is enough time to reach the bridge."

"Right."

Which meant he had to exit the hatch, yelling like a maniac and waving the meat cleaver. With the blanket over his shoulder so he could climb, he felt a bit like a caveman. But not even they had to deal with dinosaurs.

He drew in a breath, then started yelling at them to get off the boat. His feet hit the deck, and he screamed some more. Part fear, part adrenaline. He swung his gaze over the deck, searching for the biggest threat as Emma came up behind him.

All the dinosaurs were the same as the orange ones in the mess, but there must have been a dozen of them. Enough to take him down if they chose to. Right now, they were acting like startled pigeons and backing away. Their heads bobbed and their jaws opened and closed as they tried to decide what to make of this strange new animal.

Emma joined in the yelling. "Let's go."

Together they ran for the bridge. The moonlight guided their steps. After a few seconds of hesitation, the dinosaurs became braver. They saw through the act and decided that the two humans might be worth a bite, so they gave chase. They were scrabbling and scratching and making some god-awful noise that Jack didn't even know how to describe.

There were more dinosaurs than he'd first noticed. They appeared out of every dark shadow and seemed to be racing them to the door of the bridge.

Behind him, Emma swore.

"You okay?"

"I hurt my foot when I kicked one."

The door to the bridge hung open and three of the spiky feathered things hopped over the chair and the controls. A packet of crisps had been ripped open and scattered all over the floor. What other treats did Paul have stashed in here?

With the doorway now blocked by him and Emma, the dinosaurs in the bridge stared at them and fluffed their feathers.

Emma gave him a shove into the room. "Get in, they're getting brave out here."

He stumbled through the doorway and she shut the door behind them with a sigh.

"There's three in here," Jack muttered without taking his gaze off them.

She peered around him. "Oh."

"I can herd them out and you can open the door for them."

"And risk letting more in, no."

"We can't leave them in here." They were stepping on the controls and had chewed on the wheel. There was shit on the chair, and who knew what other surprises were waiting for them. "We need to clear out the room and lock the door."

He didn't want them working out how to open a door. Surely they wouldn't and he was overreacting, but the way their luck was going…

There was a commotion on the other side of the door. Squabbling and scratching like the rest were trying to get in.

Emma locked the door as if she'd been having the same thoughts as him. At least this door was sturdy. If not for the dinosaurs, this would be the safest part of the ship. But if they couldn't shoo the dinosaurs out, how were they going to remove them?

He glanced at the meat clever in his hand and then at the closest animal. He'd never hurt an animal.

"You could try grabbing one and throwing it out the window?" Emma asked.

"Yeah." That seemed better than hacking one up. He handed over the cleaver to her and then opened the blanket. Catch one and toss it out. It sounded easy. He leaned over and flicked the catch on the window to the side, but didn't push it open yet. He didn't want those outside to realize there was another way in.

Grab and shove. He had a nice thick blanket. How hard could it be?

He lunged at the closest dinosaur. It squawked, but he had it. It wriggled and clawed—their talons were mean, like meat hooks on their toes—tearing through the blanket. He barely had hold of it, and he was sure it was trying to bite him.

As he reached the window, something crashed into his leg. Pain raked down his calf.

"Get back, you little fuck," Emma snarled.

He didn't know if the grunt was Emma's or the dino's, and he didn't have time to care as he thrust his angry bundle out the window, remembering at the last moment to keep hold of the blanket. The dinosaur tumbled onto the deck and landed with a sickening splat. For a moment he hoped he hadn't killed it. Then he hoped he had. What kind of person was he becoming?

When he turned, Emma was having a kicking battle with the other two. And she was losing. Jack lunged for one and missed. He threw his arm up to avoid getting a talon to the eye, then punched it in the head. While it was stunned, he managed to grab it and send it out the window. He didn't stop to see where it landed or if it got up and walked away.

"Ow," Emma yelped.

The last one had latched onto her foot. Its jaws were clamped around her sneaker. She swung her leg at the wall. The dinosaur went limp. Jack prised its jaws open, then threw it out to join its friends. He shut the window and drew in a couple of deep breaths. It was only then he peered down to see if the broken bodies of the dinosaurs were on the deck. There was nothing there. The bastards must have shaken off the fall and scampered off.

He stepped back and shook his head before turning to Emma. She sat on the floor, blood blooming on the toe of her sneaker.

"There should be a first aid kit in here." They could patch their wounds and then make the return trip. On the other side of the door, the noise intensified. "Do you think they can smell the blood, or are they pissed that we attacked them?"

"I don't know." She started undoing her shoe. "Your leg looks pretty bad."

His leg? He glanced down and saw the blood running over his calf. "Shit."

He'd forgotten that one of them had attacked him, and he hadn't felt the pain until he'd looked. The cut was jagged, and no doubt filthy and filled with bacteria his body didn't know how to fight.

He rummaged around beneath the console until he found the first aid kit. With his prize in hand, he carefully sat on the floor with Emma. Crisps crunched beneath him. He popped open the case and nestled amongst the bandages and antiseptic was a small bottle of rum. He held it up. "Do think it's Paul's?"

"If it's not yours, definitely." She wriggled her toes. "The shoe saved my toes." But her foot was still scratched and bleeding from the sharp teeth. "Give me the kit and let me have a look at your leg."

He turned and stretched out his leg so she could see the gash. "One of their talons must have hooked me."

"I know. It was quicker than I was. Sorry."

"It's okay." At least, he hoped it would be. This was a bit different from being bitten by a dog. He sucked in a breath as she wiped antiseptic over the wound, then bandaged it. "Do you think we should be saving those supplies…"

He couldn't finish the sentence. Didn't want to because that would mean admitting that they might be stuck here. Wherever here was. But given that they were surrounded by dinosaurs, in a Mediterranean they didn't recognize, he was beginning to think they'd somehow gone back in time.

When Emma didn't answer, he turned around to look at her. "I didn't mean to sound so…grim."

"No, you're right. This might be it. In which case the first aid kit and that bottle of rum aren't going to be enough for all of us, anyway." She gave him a tight smile.

"There's another first aid kit below, and you have some wine and beers for the guests."

"Yeah, still not enough for five people stuck in the past with dinosaurs who are all too happy to see if we taste good."

So Emma had reached a similar conclusion. "You think we really are in the past?"

She shrugged. "I don't have a better theory, do you?"

"No. I just don't know how it was possible." He moved to sit next to her and held her hand. "I think we showed them we aren't easy targets."

"They were small, Jack. I'm worried about the big ones. The ones the size of buses. The ones in the water that are bigger than the boat." Her teeth raked over her lower lip as she frowned. "I'm scared, but I can't say that in front of Noah and Oliver. We have to act like we know what we're doing and that we'll get them home safe."

"And then we'll get our asses hauled over the coals." But at least they'd be home. Even if they said it was his fault and sent him to jail for ten years, it still seemed like a pretty good trade as there'd be no dinosaurs.

She nodded. "But no one could've predicted this."

Or had they, but no one had listened because it was too outlandish. The kind of thing that only turned up on conspiracy websites. "We were just unlucky."

The door rattled as the dinos on the other side kept trying to break in. Emma scowled. "They're persistent."

"Yeah, as long as they aren't successful, I'll take that as a win." Jack rolled the blanket up into a pillow they could share. "I think we're sleeping here, unless you want to make a run for it?"

She glanced around the bridge. It wasn't the most secure structure, but it was designed to be watertight and to keep would-be thieves out. It was probably more secure than the cabins.

Jack lay down and put his arm out so she could curl up next to him. "Do you think there's many of the dinos below deck, trying to get into the cabins?"

"I hope everyone down there has the good sense to keep their doors shut."

CHAPTER 8

Oliver was tempted to put headphones on so he could sleep. The party on the deck hadn't stopped and the snarls and scrabbles of claws were setting his teeth on edge, but he didn't want to be oblivious if they started trying to break into his cabin. Getting eaten by dinosaurs in his sleep wasn't how he wanted to die—not that he'd put much thought into how he wanted to die.

Until today, he hadn't thought about it at all. However, getting killed by dinosaurs was pretty much the last way he wanted to die.

He must have drifted off at some point because yelling, human yelling, startled him awake. He sat up and for a moment he couldn't work out where he was or what was going on. Growls and pained cries filled the air.

His heart thumped hard as adrenaline coursed through him. He should get up and help. But he didn't move. Wasn't sure he could.

What kind of animal made noises like that?

If he wanted to find out, he had to get up and do something to help the person screaming. What if it was Noah?

With that thought, he nodded to himself, firming his conviction. He picked up his laptop, as it was the only weapon he had. Then, holding his laptop in one hand, he cracked open his cabin door.

Something small and spiky ran past him too fast for him to see what it was. He slammed the door shut just as fast and before it could see him.

What the hell was that?

Some kind of bird was all his mind could offer up.

The screaming continued.

No, it wasn't a bird. Birds had feathers, but birds didn't snarl, and they didn't attack people. It was a dinosaur.

"Shit." If that were him out there, he'd want someone to help.

What if Noah had gone to Jack's room after Oliver had refused to answer? And now he was being attacked trying to sneak back to his room? Noah wouldn't…would he? For a second, he considered leaving Noah to suffer.

But it may not be Noah.

"Fuck." He couldn't do nothing.

He opened the door and carefully peered out. There was nothing in the corridor this time. At one end were the stairs that led to the deck, at the other was the passageway that led to the staff quarters, and that's where the screams were coming from. Without the crew, they were definitely fucked because he couldn't drive the boat even if his life depended on it—which it might. That was enough for him to screw the small amount of bravery he could muster and step out of his room. He made it as far as Noah's cabin and knocked on the door. He needed to know if it was Noah out there, and if it wasn't, Noah could join the rescue mission.

"You in there, Noah?" he whispered.

His heart pounded in his throat as he waited for Noah to answer, or for the dinosaurs to come bolting around the corner to him. The person, a man, he thought, kept screaming. Noah wasn't answering. Was he dying?

Oliver couldn't wait any longer. He turned away and started toward the passage that linked crew and guest quarters.

He regretted not telling Henry to jam it, and that he didn't want to go on a stupid cruise with him and his girlfriend. He hadn't wanted to at first, but he'd let himself be talked into it. The same way he let himself be talked into all kinds of things.

"What are you doing?" Noah said behind him.

Oliver jumped and spun. "Going to help. Coming?"

He was relieved that Noah was in his cabin, that he wasn't being attacked, and that he hadn't gone after Jack despite his obvious interest.

Noah grabbed his arm. "Don't."

Oliver stared at him. The man kept screaming and swearing, which at least meant he was alive. "We have to help."

"No, we don't. We stay in our cabins and wait for the crew to tell us what to do."

"And what if they are all dead? What do we do then? Can you drive this thing? Do you know how to survive until rescue?" While he wanted to be rescued, he didn't think it would actually happen. It was more likely that they'd be eaten by dinosaurs of one type or another, or starve to death first. "I'm going to help. You can hide if you want."

He sounded much braver than he felt. He pulled his arm free and walked away, hoping that his knees would hold him and that he wouldn't sweat so much that the laptop slid out of his hand. He grabbed the charging cable with his other hand, hoping that if he swung it, the plug would do some damage—it wasn't like he needed his laptop millions of years before they'd been invented.

He was almost at the corner when the screaming became more of a smothered gurgle. That was worse.

Was he too late? He shouldn't have dithered; he shouldn't have stopped to talk to Noah. He glanced behind. Noah was in the doorway, unable to commit.

Oliver steeled himself to first peek, then run around the corner. Before he could hesitate again, he stepped up and peered around. Nothing. The passageway was empty. He blew out a couple of quick breaths, then edged along the short passageway. A braver man would be there already. A braver man would have rushed to help immediately instead of dithering.

A bright orange, spiky feathered thing streaked past him, with something flapping out of its mouth. Was that a finger?

His stomach bucked and hot bile rose in his throat. Another one of those creatures bolted by; its blood-stained muzzle filled with something meaty.

The screaming was only a whimper now.

Or was the noise of his heartbeat drowning everything else out?

Oliver looked around the last corner. A dozen of those knee high dinosaurs were all over someone. They plucked, and the man flailed, trying to bat them away, but they just kept coming back as if they didn't feel his feeble blows.

The dinosaurs ripped at his clothes, now stained with blood. They ripped at his skin, tearing off chunks. He watched as one gulped down a chunk of flesh.

Oliver's stomach twisted, and he vomited on the floor, drawing their attention.

Oh shit.

He swung the cable. "Piss off." His voice shook, so he tried again, louder. "Piss off! Shoo!"

Two came closer, no doubt hoping to take a bite. The plug smacked one in the head, and it fell over. The other one scampered back, its claws clicking on the wooden flooring. They were afraid of him.

He wiped his mouth with the back of his hand, courage bolstered. He could do this.

All he had to do was drag the man into the room and shut the little fuckers out. But he couldn't do that while he was holding his laptop. Another one ran at him, and he swung the cable at its head. It connected, but it watched him instead of running away.

The other one was smart. As he wound up for another strike, it latched onto the cable. Oliver yelped, then swung the cable and dinosaur at the wall. The beast connected with a thud and dropped off, falling to the floor. With his attacker's attention divided, the man was dragging himself backward, toward the nearest door.

Oliver's throat closed, and he fought the urge to empty his stomach again. Half of his face was missing, ripped off, and eaten. Oliver swallowed, forcing down bile. It was Paul, the captain. They needed him alive. "Hurry up, I'll be the distraction."

And hopefully he wouldn't get eaten.

Paul edged back, even though the dinosaurs were still latching on and trying to eat him. He didn't bother to bat them away.

Oliver did. He started smacking them on the head with his laptop. Using it like a bat to hit them up the corridor like he was playing cricket. Only this time it was lives, not runs and bragging rights, at stake.

A bloody trail marked Paul's slow progress.

The dinosaurs became agitated, as if they could sense their meal was getting away and it was Oliver's fault. The noises they were making changed, and Oliver knew he was in trouble. The next attack was more than the one or two he'd been dealing with. Three came at him; as he dealt with the first two, the other one lashed out with its toe talons, raking his shin and shredding his skin.

"You shit." He smashed his laptop down so hard on its head something cracked. The laptop or the dinosaur's skull?

He couldn't stand here and wait for Paul to get clear. He needed to start backing up, so that he wasn't their next meal. He already knew no one would come to help him.

Where were Jack and Emma?

Why weren't they fighting off dinosaurs?

"Help!" he shouted. Maybe Noah would do something. Noah was great at a party, fun and all that, but when it came to anything else, Oliver had always known that he was flaky at best. At the time, though, all he'd wanted was fun.

He liked Noah; he really did. But not helping in a dinosaur emergency? That might be a deal breaker he never knew he had.

Oliver crept backwards. He didn't want to move faster than Paul, but the moment Paul got that door closed, Oliver was next on the menu. With the distance widening, the overly bright and well-armed creatures had a choice to make, and they seemed to be discussing it in chitters and growls.

How smart were they?

Sweat trickled down his spine. When he was a kid, his parents had taken him to a farm stay so he could feed the chickens, pet the sheep, and ride the pony. Henry had hated the whole thing. Oliver had loved it. This was nothing like feeding the chickens, or even like going into the coop to gather their eggs. While chickens were curious, they weren't vicious, and they weren't this smart. These animals were more like a starving pack of dogs. There was too much intelligence in their dark eyes.

And far too much chatter amongst them.

"Shut up. Get off the boat, you're trespassing." He kept shouting, saying anything that came to mind. He called them ugly, like half-plucked Christmas turkeys, and he swung the damaged cable to keep them back.

They were losing interest in him and turning back to Paul, who was halfway through the door. If he didn't hurry, he'd be locking himself in with company.

Oliver's foot skidded in his puke. He dropped to his knee. Several heads turned to look. He scrambled up, narrowly missing getting a talon to the face. They only had two moves, dart in and bite, or kick. He didn't want to end up like Paul with his face chewed off.

Paul kicked at a few that tried to follow, putting up a fight that he'd lose without medical care. There was too much blood on the floor.

Oliver took a few more swipes at the dinosaurs with his laptop. Then, as Paul shut the door, Oliver turned and ran. The dinosaurs ran after him, their long toenails scrabbling over the floor. His heart was going to burst. He ran into his cabin and slammed the door, but it jammed on one of them.

The dinosaurs squawked and hissed. Oliver pushed harder on the door. What if one squeezed through the slim gap?

Keeping his weight on the door, he smacked it with his laptop several times until it went quiet. Then he eased up on the door enough to shove the body back into the corridor before shutting his door. For several seconds, it was all he could do to breathe. His hands shook and there was blood on the gray case of the laptop. He closed his eyes and slid to the floor.

On the other side of the door, the dinosaurs ran back and forth. They'd lost their meals.

He opened his eyes. For the moment, he was safe. But he was going to need water and food at some point. What was he going to do if they were out there patrolling the corridor?

What were any of them going to do?

CHAPTER 9

Sunlight slicing through his eyelids woke Jack. He was crunched up on the floor, with his shoulder and hip taking all his weight. He rolled over with a groan as he remembered why he was on the floor and not in his bed. Then he became aware of the way his leg throbbed with every heartbeat.

Emma sat up and rubbed her eyes. "What time is it?"

He checked his watch automatically before realizing it didn't matter. Nothing here would obey the arbitrary rules of hours and minutes. Or even days of the week. Every day was survival day, but he answered anyway. "It's just after six."

"I suppose we should get up."

"Yeah." He was not looking forward to leaving the safety of the bridge, but he needed to piss and aside from the rum there was nothing to drink. He stood and offered Emma his hand. "It sounds quiet out there."

She tilted her head as she listened. "Are they gone?"

He wasn't that hopeful. Even if they were gone today, he was sure they'd be back tonight if they didn't leave and find a new place to berth the boat.

They peered out the windows, but couldn't see anything moving. Not even a human. He swallowed his fears. There was no need to feed them and give them strength. He picked up the blanket and left the knife and machete to Emma. "I'll go first?"

She nodded, and he didn't waste time. The longer he waited, the worse it would be, so he pulled open the door a good six inches. Nothing came running.

He bathed in those few seconds of relief before opening the door wider. Nothing moved on the deck, so he stepped into the doorway.

The deck was deserted and for a few heartbeats he was almost able to convince himself that he'd imagined it all. But a few of the odd feathers and some shit marred the deck, proving that there had in fact been dinosaurs on deck. "All clear."

They left the bridge, and he made sure to lock it, then they crept toward the hatch. Emma tugged at his sleeve. "Look."

He lifted his gaze to see where she was pointing. Over the sea there were birds; no, he realized with horror, they were pterosaurs. And they were huge. One dove toward the water and he watched as it hit the water and plucked out a fish that was easily as big as him.

Emma swore. "Is everything here hungry?"

"Yes." Including him. "Let's move faster and we can have some breakfast while we figure out what to do."

"We need to find a way home."

She wasn't wrong. But he had no idea how to do that.

He tossed the blanket over his shoulder and started down the ladder. He'd expected people to be up, but maybe they'd slept better than him. His feet touched the floor, and he paused. Something smelled terrible.

Emma stopped halfway down. "It smells like blood."

There were scratches on the floor and animal shit. "The orange bastards were down here too."

"Are they still down here?"

"I don't know." He wanted to run back up the stairs. Not that it was any safer. "We'll move carefully." And quietly. The last thing he wanted was to surprise a pack of them and start the day with a fight.

His heartbeat echoed is his ears as he padded along the corridor. He rapped on the door of the first cabin. "All good in there?" he whispered as loud as he dared.

"Yes."

"Stay where you are." Jack moved on to the next cabin and repeated the process.

The door opened, and Oliver peered out. "Are they gone?"

"I don't know. Stay in your cabin until we come back."

Oliver hesitated. "They attacked Paul."

"What?" Emma asked too loudly.

Jack tried not to cringe.

"I heard someone screaming and went out to help. There were about a dozen of them, eating him." His voice hitched.

"Eating him?" Jack stared at Oliver. Yes, they had pointy teeth and oversized toenails, but they were small. They couldn't eat a whole human…could they?

Oliver nodded. "Tearing at him." He pointed up the hallway. "I distracted them so he could escape, but he was in bad shape. They're vicious." He stuck his leg out. "I got scratched."

"We had a run in with them last night too. We'll patch you up in a bit, okay." He pointed at his bandaged leg and tried not to think about getting mobbed by the dinosaurs and pulled apart bit by bit. His stomach tightened. "Where was Paul when you last saw him?"

"He went into the bathroom…the heads."

"Okay, shut your door and wait."

Oliver did as he was told. Jack glanced at Emma. Emma's lips were pressed together, and her face was pale, as though she was already expecting the worst. Jack wasn't sure which was worse, that Paul was alive and gravely injured with no help coming, or that he was dead. Either way, it put Jack in charge. And while that was something he'd wanted for a long time, this was not how he wanted it, or when he wanted it.

He didn't know how to deal with dinosaurs or how to get everyone home. That was of course assuming that they had gone back in time—which was as impossible as dinosaurs suddenly appearing in his time or becoming lost in the Mediterranean after being hit by a freak wave. Nothing made sense anymore.

"Come on." Emma gave him a nudge. "We need to help Paul."

"Yeah." And what if they couldn't? They had a few bandages and some antiseptic cream. If he'd been half eaten by the spiky orange things, there wasn't much they could do.

The corridor was clear, but they moved slowly. Jack was listening for the tapping, scrabbling sound of the orange dinosaurs, but all he heard was the gentle slap of waves on the side of the boat. Nothing different to normal. He wanted to believe that it had all been a nightmare, but there was too much evidence that it was real—including puddles of piss, logs of shit, and gouges in the floor. He stopped just before the corridor made a ninety-degree turn toward the staff quarters because he could hear breathing that wasn't his or Emma's.

He touched his ear. Emma nodded and wrinkled her nose. He smelled it too, the stink of blood and now familiar reek of dinosaur. He was sure that Paul and the dinosaurs were round the corner and he wasn't ready to face either with only the blanket and Emma's knives. He breathed in and out, then leaned forward to peer around the corner, while praying that there was nothing waiting to pounce at him.

His gaze skimmed over the blood-streaked and scratched floor. He didn't know if it was human or dino blood, but there was a lot. There were small white and red chunks on the floor. It took a moment for him to realize they were bits of bone. Jack gritted his teeth and forced himself to keep looking.

Pressed up against the door to the staff heads were about six of the orange spiky dinosaurs. This close it was clear they were dinosaurs. Some kind of speedy two-legged meat eating variety. Their skin was streaky orange and brown, and their feathers were also bright, making them seem like prehistoric parrots.

Deadly parrots.

Even while sleeping, they seemed dangerous. Their hooked claws were stained with blood, as were their muzzles. But they were sleeping, so maybe they were nocturnal. However, that didn't mean they wouldn't wake and attack if they thought they were in danger. With the dinosaurs sleeping by the door, they couldn't reach Paul.

Shit.

He backed up and motioned Emma back down the corridor. He didn't stop until they were in the galley, well away from where the guests might hear, but he still kept his voice low.

Emma scowled at him. "What's going on?"

"There's six of them by the door, guarding Paul." To get to Paul, they had to remove the dinosaurs. This was not a problem he'd ever been trained in. Logically, he should radio for help and head for shore.

He scrubbed his hand over his face. No one had briefed him on what to do if the boat accidentally travelled backward in time. Die was the short answer. Survival was much harder.

"What should we do? We can't leave them there."

For a moment, Jack was tempted to say they could. He'd untie the boat and they could race across the sea to anywhere but here. There had to be other humans. He forced himself to breathe. "The two guests are safe. And there's nothing on the deck. We could try calling for help, or even searching for help.

In daylight we might see something that we missed. Maybe there's a portal…"

Emma stared at him. "Paul needs help now."

"And we can't provide it. There was too much blood." And bits of bone…

"And when they wake, trapping everyone in their rooms?"

He clenched his jaw. "I don't know."

She shook her head. "We need to help Paul, now. We can call for help after."

"He might be dead."

"He might be alive," she countered.

Jack closed his eyes. They couldn't kill one dinosaur without waking the others and when angered, they were ferocious. "There's a porthole in the head. We could try to reach him that way, at least to check in on him."

"Okay. I can do that. And if he's alive, I'll smash it and help him." She didn't sound very convinced.

"There are more dinosaurs out than in. I should do it."

"You're the only one who can operate the boat. Besides, I'll be quick."

The dinosaurs would probably be quicker. Why couldn't they have arrived in a nice herd of herbivores, instead of a critter infested mangrove swamp? Aside from the pterosaurs, he hadn't taken a good look around at where they were. Perhaps it was peaceful out there. It wasn't like the Earth had been packed with dinosaurs, had it? "Let's see what's out there before we make any other plans. We might be able to raise another ship or a town or something."

"Yeah, we can't be the only ones." Emma picked up the first aid kit from the kitchen and slipped it over her shoulder. "Maybe all the animals are nocturnal around here. It's bloody hot already."

"Most things hunt at dawn and dusk, right?"

"I think so. So if we explore at midday or midnight…"

Jack nodded, even though they were both spinning bullshit. At least they were telling each other the same lies.

CHAPTER 10

Oliver took a last sip from his drink bottle. Now he was out of water, and he was starving. The water in the bathroom in his cabin wasn't for drinking, and he didn't know if it was recycled or seawater, and he didn't want to give himself the shits by finding out.

Jack and Emma hadn't returned, and it had been at least half an hour.

But there'd been no screaming either, so he figured they hadn't been attacked. His leg throbbed. The scratches were probably infected. How long until it spread and killed him? He figured that was days away, and his body might successfully fight it off. What he needed was some antiseptic from the first aid kit to give his body a chance. Or was it already too late? He'd washed the wounds with water, but that wasn't good enough—he didn't know what the dinosaurs had on their giant toenails, only that it wouldn't be anything good.

After another five minutes had passed in silence—aside from some movement on deck—he decided to risk leaving his cabin. He cracked open the door and when the corridor was empty, he made his way to the kitchen. He was sure there was supposed to be a first aid kit in there, but he couldn't find it.

He muttered a curse, then helped himself to a banana and some milk. The fridge was cold, but for how much longer? Surely the boat's battery couldn't last forever, not that he knew anything about boats. The food didn't settle his stomach, but it didn't make him feel worse either. He was blaming everything on being a few million years out of synch. This couldn't be good for the body. Was it messing with his internal organs? Giving him cancer?

Banging overhead made him glance up and his heart race.

Where were Jack and Emma?

He needed them, or at least Jack, to get home.

He picked up the heaviest frying pan in the kitchen—an improvement on his now rather dented and cracked laptop—and made his way up the ladder. Cautiously he stuck his head up, half expecting it to be bitten off, but all he saw was the brilliant blue of the sky, and the green leaves of the trees they were nestled beneath.

Just because he couldn't see any dinosaurs didn't mean they weren't out there—unless he'd had one hell of a hallucination last night. Maybe it had been, and he'd scratched his leg on something mundane. Yeah, that sounded a lot more reasonable than dinosaurs.

Yet, as he glanced over the deck and saw feathers and blood, he knew he hadn't dreamed it all. He stepped onto the deck, frying pan at the ready. He wasn't going anywhere unarmed, and he would not be an easy meal.

For a few seconds, he was the only human in existence. There was nothing but the sounds of wind in the trees, the buzzing of insects and calling of animals he couldn't even name. He stared at the trees, knowing that there was life in there even if he couldn't see it. Gradually he was able to see the rapid movements of small creatures on the branches. A smile curved his lips. It wasn't all hellish, and he wished he'd grabbed his phone to take some photos. But he didn't see any dinosaurs. Weren't they supposed to be kings of the Cretaceous or something?

Shouldn't they be everywhere?

"What was that?" Emma asked.

Oliver spun, not sure where she was. He made his way round the deck to the other side of the bridge.

Jack was standing on the deck, peering over at something. "I don't know, hurry up."

"What are you doing?" Oliver walked over.

Jack startled, like he'd been bitten. "What are you doing out of your cabin?"

"You were taking too long. Besides, I was careful."

"Where's Noah?" Jack jerked his chin in a rough nod.

"In his cabin." He needed Jack to know that Noah wasn't going to be of any use in an emergency. "He didn't even try to help Paul last night, he was too scared."

Jack sighed. "He was smart. I don't want to be storing bodies. You might have been killed."

Yeah, but he'd only realized that when he was already ass deep. "If I'd done nothing, Paul would be dead."

"He might still be dead." Jack peered over the side. "Anything?"

Oliver edged closer to the railing and saw Emma dangling from a rope, trying to open a window. "Is that what you're trying to find out...why didn't you open the door?"

Jack gave him a look that suggested Oliver should've kept his mouth shut. "Because there are dinosaurs guarding it."

Oliver stepped back. "They're still down there?"

"Yes." Jack lifted his gaze to the sky, where a few birds that weren't actual birds soared. "You still okay?"

"Yes," Emma said from off the side of the ship.

Oliver's gaze drifted over the water. It was crystal clear, like looking through glass to what was on the bottom. He had no idea how deep it was, only that there were tree roots and shells and tiny fish, all things that appeared very familiar. Like this was some kind of extreme nature tour that he hadn't signed up for.

He almost wanted to hop on a jet ski and explore. Then he remembered what had happened to Henry and Tahlia. There were big things in the water, even if he couldn't see them right now.

"Wait, I can see him. Or part of him." She banged on the window while Jack and Oliver watched. "Paul! Move your leg if you can hear me."

Oliver held his breath.

"There's a lot of blood on the floor, Jack," she called.

"Can you break the glass? Or remove it?"

"Even if I could, I won't fit through." She banged on the glass again and shouted more loudly.

The noise made the life in the trees around them go quiet.

The hair on Oliver's arms spiked up like he was freezing, not sweating his ass off. The silence was worse than the chatter. Oliver glanced around, not sure what he was expecting, only that it wouldn't be anything good.

Jack swore. "I'm pulling you up. Oliver, help me."

Oliver grabbed the rope and they hauled Emma up. He didn't know why and didn't ask. As Emma climbed over the railing, he saw the ripple in the water as a huge fin, more like a sail, broke the surface.

"Get back and get down." Jack pushed him and Oliver dropped to the deck.

The creature hit the boat and made it sway.

That was not the same thing that had taken Henry. "What was that?"

Jack didn't get the chance to answer as the creature launched out of the water, its claws caught on the railing as it pulled itself up.

Dark green and gray, it was huge, like an oversized crocodile with a sail on its back. The three of them scrambled back, as it landed on the deck with a crash that tipped the boat enough to make them slide toward its head and its parted jaws that were lined with far too many pointed teeth.

Oliver grabbed the first thing his fingers found and held on. This was no different to rock climbing, hold on or fall, but this time he had no safety harness and there was a mouth waiting to catch him. His heart bounced in his throat. They were going to capsize and be dinner.

Everything not tied down slid toward the railing and fell into the sea, including Oliver's frying pan. Jack grabbed Emma's hand.

The boat hung for what felt like hours. The monster snapped its jaws, hooked its back leg over the now warped railing, and pushed further onto the deck. The extra weight broke the spell and the boat hit the water and tipped the other way for a second before stabilizing with the creature firmly on board.

Oliver scrambled farther back while he could, seeking something to hold on to and a way to escape. The only place to go was off the boat and into the trees, but he wasn't sure that was any safer.

Emma frantically fiddled with something at her waist.

The rope that had held her safe while over the side was now trapping her within the monster's reach, Oliver realized with horror. His gaze flicked between Emma and the beast. The creature's name rose out of Oliver's mind, Spinosaurus.

The sail on its back gave it away. He should've realized sooner. But knowing the name didn't help Emma.

"Where's the knife?" Jack yelled as he desperately searched the deck.

The dinosaur bellowed and launched forward, grabbing Emma in its jaws. It jerked its head once, then crunched, and blood spattered the deck. It swallowed, and she was gone. The end of the rope hung out of its mouth as its dark eyes watched Jack and Oliver as if deciding which one to eat next. Jack was closer, but he knew how to drive the boat.

Shit, he needed to distract it.

"Hey, you big, ugly, overgrown lump. What do you think you're doing?" Oliver jumped up and down, trying to draw it away from Jack. Oliver wasn't far from the hatch; he could go below deck…where there were more dinosaurs. And the weight of this one was breaking up the deck, anyway. It must be like parking a bus on board. "Jack, get away!"

Jack blinked and glanced at him. The monster lurched closer to Jack, ripping up the deck with every clawed step. Would it fall through and crush those below?

After another heartbeat, Jack stumbled back, putting valuable inches between him and the Spinosaurus. The beast was not deterred. It had made the effort to board, and now it wanted to eat whatever it could manage.

A wave of despair hit Oliver, and he didn't think he'd be able to escape the terrible crush. He was going to die. It was a matter of when, not if. For a moment, he envied Henry's bravery. He'd died with hope, and the belief that he was right. That had to be better than surviving one nightmare, only to wake and find another one waiting.

"What do we do?" he called out, hoping that Jack had an answer.

"I don't know." Jack stared at the beast. "It ate Emma."

"It's going to eat us if we don't move." Oliver looked up at the overhanging branches. He'd take his chances in the trees. He took a short run up and jumped. His fingers closed around a branch which had more flex than he was happy with, but then was up and moving closer toward the trunk.

Below, Jack remained on the busted deck, only meters from the dinosaur that had decided humans made an easy dinner.

CHAPTER 11

Jack's mind kept replaying the way the dinosaur had casually plucked Emma off the deck and swallowed her with barely a pause. Like she didn't matter and was just another meal waiting to be eaten.

Logically he knew he had to do something, but what could he do against a creature that was as long as the boat? Its tail was hanging off the side and its weight was breaking the ship. He was a minnow. Completely irrelevant to the beast, unless he was in its jaws.

They watched each other.

It reminded him of the crocodiles he'd seen at a zoo once. They'd been still and calm until the keeper had thrown a chicken into the enclosure, then it had been all teeth and claws. The stillness hid the cruel intelligence of the animals. There were signs on the enclosures about not getting too close and how one had escaped by climbing the fencing. It had seemed impossible, not anymore, after watching this thing climb onto the boat.

And this dinosaur was far bigger than any crocodile.

The sail on its back rippled, the only sign that it was alive.

Jack didn't move. He was sure it could see him; it was staring right at him, but he was equally sure that if he moved first, it would close the distance and he'd be next to be swallowed. He took one breath and then another, hoping that he'd figure something out before the dinosaur did.

While he'd seen skeletons in museums, they had never seemed this big. This was bus big, and it was breathing its rotten breath all over him. He wanted to gag, to run, to break down and cry, but he couldn't do anything.

"Jack, edge slowly back from the Spinosaurus and climb up here." Oliver's voice drifted toward him, but if he risked a glance and took his gaze off the beast, it would be on him. Its legs were as long as him; it could cover distances in speeds that he couldn't even imagine.

It wasn't the same creature that had eaten Henry and Tahlia, and the jet ski though. That hadn't had a sail on its back, and Oliver had called it something else.

It was stupid to think there was only one predator in the sea. This sea was much bigger than the Mediterranean he knew. He forced his foot to slide backward.

While a blanket might have worked on the little orange fuckers, it wasn't going to work on this thing. No, that would be like throwing a tissue on a snarling dog.

Even the knife and cleaver, that were now lost over the edge, wouldn't have done much good. Its hide was scarred from attacks by other dinosaurs and its teeth were bigger than the knife. The only thing they had that might damage this beast was fuel and fire.

But that meant getting close enough to douse it, and light it, without setting fire to himself, or the boat, or getting eaten.

He didn't like his odds.

He took another tiny step back.

The beast blinked. It had noticed that lunch was thinking about escaping. Its claws flexed against the deck of the boat, but otherwise didn't move.

It would be quick if it ate him. One chomp. Better than being nibbled to death. He was sure there were a hundred other ways to die here that were worse. But he wasn't ready to start choosing the best way to die. He wanted to go home, even though there was nothing good waiting for him there either.

"You have to move," Oliver called.

The beast's gaze flicked upward to where Oliver must be.

"Where are you?"

"In a tree. Turn to your left and sprint. You'll need to pull yourself up and the branch will bend."

That at least gave him direction. He drew in a breath, knowing it could be his last, and did exactly as Oliver had told him. His feet slapped the deck as he ran. The branch was overhead.

The dino roared, and the boat lurched as it moved. Jack jumped and grabbed the branch, pulling his legs up as fast as he could. Then he was staring into the maw of the beast. His weight made the branch bend, and he dropped closer to the waiting teeth.

If it broke…

The jaws slammed shut, and it fell back onto the deck, splinting the wood and sending the boat rocking. Jack hugged the branch, unable to move. He squeezed his eyes shut. His muscles were locked in place.

Below, the beast moved, grunting, and making other noises that should be alien, but were too familiar. The creatures here might be millions of years old, but nature seemed to repeat successful ideas.

He cracked one eye open; sure enough it was watching him.

"Move back here. It's safer," Oliver whispered like the beast would overhear and understand.

Nowhere was safer. But he forced himself to sit up and ease forward, inch by inch, until he was up against the trunk of the tree with Oliver. Oliver moved over and perched on a different branch, with a grim set to his face, like he was a hardened battle veteran who'd seen too much. Very different to the young man who had been arguing with his brother and making the most of the sunshine.

"What now?" Jack stared at the beast. They'd escaped immediate death, but it had commandeered the boat like the first pirate history had never recorded.

"I was hoping you had the rest of the plan."

Jack shook his head. All of his brave ideas of sailing straight out to sea and finding a way home, or other ships and people, were gone. He lifted his gaze from the beast to the endless ocean beyond. If not the dinosaur beneath him, it was easy to imagine this was another beautiful sunny day on the Med.

Annoyance about the stupid whale sighting burned in his veins. His mind filled with if onlys that wouldn't change anything. All he had was now. Which gave him exactly nothing.

"I'm sorry about Emma," Oliver said.

Jack swallowed the lump that formed in his throat. They'd kept it secret, which meant no one knew that the loss bit deeper. "She's my girlfriend."

"Oh…I didn't know."

He leaned back against the tree trunk. Insects as big as his hand moved through the leaves. Below in the water life went on. Most of the animals here didn't care about the misplaced humans. The tide had come in during the night, meaning the beast was able to swim up, but if it hadn't been in, they would've never been able to reach the branches.

"You weren't supposed to. We weren't supposed to be dating. But a few months ago it just kind of happened." One of those things that they'd both been aware of, and for a little while they'd tried to avoid before giving in. Giving in to the attraction had been so easy, it had felt right.

Oliver smiled. "I understand how that happens. Noah…"

"Yeah, I figured."

"How?"

Jack lifted an eyebrow. "Noah is not exactly subtle."

That and he'd dated a few guys in the past. Always secretly. He'd thought Emma might be the one, though. When he got his skippers ticket, they were going to try to move boats and work together. Then they could've been open, and a part of him had been looking forward to that. The rest of him had been terrified. What if it didn't work out?

None of that mattered now.

The plans they'd made were gone.

"Noah's still below deck."

"And Paul. As long as they stay behind closed doors, they'll be fine. Better than us. We have no water or food." It was already hot and humid, and he was sure the insects were going to start biting sooner rather than later.

Oliver pressed his lips together. "Then we need to find a way to get that oversized, frilly monster off the boat."

"And do what?" He tipped his head back and stared at the sky. "There's more than one Spinosaurus out there." More than one kind of dinosaur that wanted a taste.

"We don't know what's out there. It won't only be them."

Jack glanced at him. "Do you want to wait for rescue?"

"Do you?"

"I don't know." He didn't know anything. It was easy to dream of running when there wasn't a sodding great dinosaur on deck. "What will Noah want to do?"

"Hide in his room until it's safe to come out." Oliver sighed. "He didn't help last night. He hid. I didn't realize he was such a coward."

Jack reached out and put a hand on Oliver's thigh. "Hey, he's allowed to be scared."

"Yeah, I'm scared. But I'm not going to sit around and do nothing. That's the difference."

Oliver was right, they were all shit scared, but hiding wasn't going to change things. He wanted to say something reassuring, but had nothing. They were just going to have to deal.

The Spinosaurus turned around like it was getting comfy. Jack had no doubt that it could outwait them. They'd fall out of the tree when thirst and exhaustion overcame them. There'd be no running then.

"Waiting for rescue is as bad as running. Where are we even running to? Where are we?"

"The past," Oliver said with more conviction than Jack wanted to hear.

Jack laughed.

"I know how that sounds." Oliver hung his head. "But how else do I explain it?"

"I wasn't laughing at you. I agree. It's just…just so…"

"Yeah."

They sat in silence, Jack's mind tumbling with a hundred reasons why they couldn't be in the past, and only one that they were. The evidence was below them, digesting his girlfriend. "So what do we do?"

"There are only two options. Find a way home or find a way to survive."

Jack shook his head. "There's a third. Die."

CHAPTER 12

Oliver was sure his tongue was stuck to the roof of his mouth. His T-shirt clung to his skin with sweat and all he'd done was sit in this damn tree for what felt like all day, but the sun was only at its zenith. There was still half a day to go…and that assumed that the Spinosaurus got off the boat and went home at dusk.

But they couldn't sit here forever waiting for it to move.

Every so often he'd scan the ocean, searching for the boat that Paul had promised would come. How they were going to reach them, Oliver didn't know unless there was some kind of portal linking the present and the past. Aside from the pterosaurs hunting above the surface, and dipping in to grab their prey, and the sea creatures breaking the surface, the sea was clear of human life.

No one had seen the flare, because there was no one to see it.

Which meant no one would come.

Was the Mediterranean on alert because there was some kind of dinosaur swimming around terrorizing boats? Would the authorities assume they were the first victims? That they were dead and not bother looking?

Despair tightened its grip until it was almost too hard to breathe.

He closed his eyes against the glare but couldn't go to sleep in case he fell off the branch. If he did that, he'd end up in the water below. He didn't know how deep it was, but there were plenty of things down there doing what they did best, which seemed to be eating. He scratched at his arm where something had bitten him. It was itchy and had come up in a red welt the like someone had slapped him. It hadn't killed him yet, so he'd probably survive.

He glanced over at Jack. He hadn't spoken for a while. He just sat there staring at the dinosaur like he could will it off the boat. Though once it was off the boat what they were going to do, he didn't know. The idea of heading out in open water and searching for other boats and people didn't fill him with any hope.

"Got a plan yet?" Oliver's voice was little more than a croak.

"No."

"It would be good if we could contact Noah."

Oliver huffed out a breath. Noah was useless. "I don't think he'd help us."

"But he might help himself."

Maybe. "But he's safe."

"For the moment. When the sun sets, the orange ones will become active and want to eat."

"And? If he stays in his room, he's fine." He might have even raided the kitchen while everything was quiet.

Jack shook his head. "It means if we are going to act it needs to be in daylight."

"As soon as we climb down, that thing is going to be after us. Maybe it will leave if we wait a bit longer…" But it seemed pretty settled. "It will need more food and we aren't cooperating."

"I never thought I'd be considering the feeding habits of dinosaurs." Jack's stomach gave a grumble. "More importantly, we need to eat and drink."

Oliver nodded. His head was pounding. It was only dehydration, and it wouldn't kill him immediately, even though it felt like it was making a good attempt.

They slipped into silence again. It was easier not to talk. The heat was stifling, and his mouth was filled with cotton wool. All he wanted was a drink. The water lapping at the base of the trees clawed at him, tempting him to come and take a sip.

While it was salt water, he wondered how salty it was. Were the oceans more or less salty this far back? And if they were less salty, were they safe to drink? Would he be able to tell from tasting it?

He was never going anywhere without a drink bottle again.

Though he could imagine it rolling off the deck like everything else, leaving him in the same situation. No, it would be a worse situation as then he wouldn't have his drink bottle at all.

But there was bottled water in the fridge, and it would be cold.

"The flare gun is in the bridge," Jack said, startling Oliver.

He must have drifted off, which was dangerous given his perch above the Spinosaurus.

"That won't kill it." That won't damage its hide. It looks like a tough bastard.

"No, but the flare might scare it. And if it went down its throat, the heat would do some damage."

While that was true, there was a giant hole in Jack's plan. "One of us has to reach the bridge."

"And unlock the door to grab the gun."

"Right." That didn't seem impossible at all. "You have the key?"

Jack touched a bunch of keys clipped to his shorts. "We also have fuel for the jet skis. Jet ski."

"And?" Oliver asked, even though he saw where Jack was going with this plan.

"And maybe it will chomp on the jerry can, then toss in a match and we can have barbequed dinosaur."

Oliver didn't fancy eating the beast, and he wasn't sure if the fuel and fire would kill it, but it might move on. "Do we have matches?"

"In the kitchen."

Oliver sighed. They'd have to split up, one getting the fuel, the other the matches. They'd both need to be successful. That plan was impossible. "Why don't we feed it the orange ones?"

"I thought of that, but it might hang around, hoping for more. Don't feed strays." Jack forced a grin. "You got anything to add to the plans, or a preference?"

"Are we trying to kill it or move it?"

"Either. We can't go anywhere with it on deck."

Oliver nodded. "And once it's moved, what do we do?"

"We run."

CHAPTER 13

"Run where?" Oliver asked.

As plans went, it wasn't much of one. Jack was well aware of that, but he hadn't come up with anything that wasn't any less reckless or with better odds of survival.

Paul's rescue had failed to show.

Paul might be dead, or he was at the very least suffering alone. Noah was stuck in his room, which wasn't much better than being up a tree. And come dusk, when the tide went out, the orange fuckers would come out to hunt and would no doubt swarm the boat again. Unless they cast off and anchored just out of the mangroves for the night. While the trees gave an illusion of safety, it was a lie.

As far as he could tell, the shallows extended a couple of meters into the trees before giving way to soggy, solid ground. He watched several different types of dinosaurs hunting deeper in the swamp. Some of them seemed to eat the insects, others moved through the tree branches—they had fortunately stayed away from the two humans.

Deeper in the swamp, the Spinosaurus wouldn't be able to follow them as it was too big. But they'd be easy targets for the orange fuckers and the other carnivores that lived in there.

"We shift the dino, then move out of the swamp. If we make a run out to sea, maybe we can get back home." All the while hoping that they weren't attacked by the mosasaurs.

Oliver nodded. "And if we can't go home?"

"We need to make a different plan." He wasn't sure if it would be better to die trying, or die trying to survive, waiting for a rescue that wouldn't come. If it wasn't here by now, it wasn't coming.

"What kind of plan?"

"We need fresh water." That was first. "Food, shelter—"

"Weapons."

Jack stared at him. "What are you going to make besides spears?"

How could they survive in a place where the predators were bigger than elephants?

"I think we should focus on the first problem." Oliver pointed at the snoozing Spinosaurus. "And I think we should preserve the flare gun."

That was a good idea. Ideally, he'd like to preserve the fuel too, but they didn't have that luxury. "So jet ski fuel and matches?"

Oliver nodded. "We'll have to take one job each."

"Yeah." And if one of them failed, it was all over. "Matches are in the galley; she keeps them in the bottom drawer." And she'd never be looking for them again. He bit the inside of his lower lip and tried not to think about it. But when he blinked, all he saw was her disappearing into the beast's mouth. "This is a trick we can only do once, because we won't have any more fuel."

There wouldn't be time to pour off some of the fuel into the spare jerry can. All he'd be able to do was grab it. He knew where it was. It shouldn't be hard. And if there wasn't a dinosaur on the deck, he'd have sauntered down there and grabbed it already.

"So I'm on matches…then what? How do we do this?"

"Fast and carefully." It was probably going to take Oliver longer to go below and grab the matches than it was for him to get the jerry can. "I'll distract it so you can make it to the hatch."

"And then what?"

Jack glanced at him. "I'll hope you're fast."

"I'm not faster than that thing."

"If I have to, I'll jump overboard and swim around to the jet ski." He stared at the water. It was so clear that he'd have enjoyed putting on flippers and snorkel if they weren't stuck in the wrong time.

"I'm not sure that's a good idea. We don't know what's down there."

"You just worry about getting below." His voice cracked. His throat was so dry even swallowing hurt. All he wanted to do was have a drink. If that meant killing the Spinosaurus first, then so be it. He eased away from the tree trunk.

Oliver sat up straight. "What? Now?"

"I'm funking thirsty and hungry, and the longer we wait the harder it will be to do this. Meanwhile it's going to be well rested." He crawled along the branch, not sure if the dino was asleep, watching them, or just listening. He didn't know how good its eyesight and hearing were, and he didn't want to find out the wrong way.

He was going to have to drop onto the deck first. Maybe if they were both quiet, they could get into position, and this would be easy. The branch bowed as Oliver followed him. Jark motioned him back a bit. They couldn't afford to mess this up.

With the tide going out, the boat was lower in the water, which meant when he dropped down, he wouldn't be able to reach the branch to climb back up. This was a one-way trip.

It had to work.

The dinosaur didn't move. He watched its flanks rise and fall with every breath. It was too still. He was sure it knew exactly what they were up to, and it was waiting for him to land on the deck before attacking.

Jack drew in a breath, then carefully lowered himself so he was hanging on by only his fingers. Once he let go…

With one eye on the beast and the other on the deck, Jack dropped. His feet hit the deck in a noise that he was sure would've woken the dinosaur even it had been sleeping half a mile away.

Its eyes cracked open.

Jack ran toward the jet ski, not stopping to see if Oliver was following. Oliver needed to wait until the dinosaur was chasing after him before making a run for the hatch.

Was it going to move?

He stopped and turned. His pulse thumped in his head like a nightclub bass.

The beast yawned as though bored with the humans. Like it wasn't hungry at all. Jack didn't trust it. He risked a glance at Oliver. He was perched near the end of the branch, waiting.

"What are you doing, you oversized crocodile?" Jack shouted. He had to draw it away.

The dino flexed its claws, tearing up part of the deck. Then it got to its feet, first all four, then all the way up onto its hind legs.

Oh shit. While he'd known it was big…it was fucking big. It seemed tall enough that if it got on its tip toes, it could pluck Oliver off the branch and gobble him up.

This might have been a mistake.

One he couldn't undo.

The Spinosaurus took a step toward Jack and the boat tilted. It was going to destroy the boat, or at the very least capsize it. The rocking seemed to piss it off. It lashed its tail, making the boat rock worse. It roared in Jack's direction as though blaming him, the rope flopping between its teeth. Jack flinched back before remembering he had a job to do. He needed the fuel.

When he glanced up at the branch, Oliver was gone.

CHAPTER 14

With the monster's back turned, Oliver dropped to the deck and ran for the hatch. He ducked under its tail and almost slid down the ladder. Only remembering halfway down that there were still dinosaurs below deck and that he had to be careful. He glanced over his shoulder, but there was nothing in the corridor.

For a second, he was tempted to bang on Noah's door and tell him to do something useful, but he had no idea what he could do besides stay out of the way. So he focussed on his job and ran into the galley.

Bottom drawer.

There were two sets of drawers. He opened one. No matches. He opened the other one. Three boxes of matches and a lighter. He pocketed the lighter and one box—so they had back up.

"What are you doing?"

Oliver spun. Noah stood in the doorway.

"Grabbing things to get the dinosaur off the deck. What are you doing?"

"I heard shouting. No one came to tell me it was safe to come out. I thought you were dead."

"Jack will be if I don't go back up there." He went to brush past.

Noah grabbed his arm. "Where have you been?"

"Hiding up a tree."

Noah's eyes narrowed for a second, like he didn't believe him.

"There's a Spinosaurus on deck. It ate Emma." He yanked his arm away. He wasn't going to let it eat Jack, too. "Instead of hiding you should have helped with the dino problem."

"I don't want to be here."

"Neither do I. But I'm not going to sit around and wait for someone to save me."

Noah's lip curled in a sneer. "You like him, that's why you're putting on a show and trying to help. He's staff."

"He's trying to save all of our asses." He pushed past, not stopping to listen to the rest of Noah's arguments. Or his apology. Was he actually sorry, or did he think that was what Oliver wanted to hear?

He didn't know what he wanted, but it wasn't that.

At the bottom of the ladder, he stopped. "Just go back to your room. I'll let you know when we're home."

Then he started climbing. The boat rocked with every step the monster took, but he could hear Jack, which was a good thing. Carefully, he stuck his head out, half expecting it to be bitten off.

The boat was tilted toward the back where Jack was. Oliver climbed the rest of the way out and ran over the splintered deck to the bridge. While it felt nice to have a wall at his back, he didn't think it would do much good.

He needed to call out and let Jack know he was back, but his mouth was dry, like he'd been licking salt all day. He should've grabbed a drink in the kitchen, but he hadn't been sure there was time.

He pursed his lips and whistled instead of talking.

The monster went still.

"Thank fuck," Jack said.

Oliver couldn't see him, but he didn't sound far away. "I'm by the bridge," he croaked.

"Stay there, I'll come to you." He did, climbing over what was left of the railing. The jerry can was strapped to him with a life jacket. "Is it looking for me?"

The boat rocked as the monster moved, trying to turn around.

"I think it heard you. And it's coming this way. I have matches and a lighter. What are you going to do?"

"Throw the jerry can and hope it eats it. Then you toss a match at the spilled fuel."

The monster roared, and its tail slammed into the bridge just over their heads as it turned. Glass shattered.

"Won't that set fire to the boat?"

"We can put out a fire more easily." Jack stepped away from the building. "You hungry?"

The monster turned its head. There was no doubt that it saw them. Its nostrils flared and its hands made little grabbing motions, like it was imagining how to pick them up and put them in its mouth.

Fuck, he needed to pull the matches out of his pocket. He did so with shaking hands. Would he be able to even strike it?

Jack tossed the jerry can at the beast.

It opened its mouth as if to take it, then jerked away. The jerry can landed on the deck and skidded between the beast's legs.

"What the hell?" Jack muttered.

Oliver didn't know what to say. Neither of them had considered the beast not wanting to eat the jerry can. "What now?"

Jack took a step back until his back was against the wall of the bridge. "We die?"

The jerry can was leaking. Oliver struck the match. Yeah, the beast hadn't eaten it, but hopefully it didn't like fire. The match burned hot and bright in his hand, then he tossed it at the fuel, willing the match to make it.

The match spun through the air and for a moment nothing happened. Then the air beneath the beast caught fire. Heat pulsed over Oliver's skin, and the spilled fuel shimmered as the flames took hold.

The Spinosaurus roared and stumbled back and onto the railing. The boat tipped from having too much weight on one side.

Oliver grabbed hold of a rope, and so did Jack.

The dinosaur, with flames licking up its legs from where it had stood in the fuel, was thrown overboard, along with the burning jerry can.

"Yes!" Oliver yelled. It had worked. The dinosaur was gone. Now they could figure out how to get home.

But as the boat levelled, and the deck was on fire, he realized their next problem was saving the ship. Without it, they weren't going anywhere.

CHAPTER 15

Flames licked across the deck, fed by the spilled fuel. The shattered wood provided easy kindling. Jack stared, transfixed by the fire. In the water, the Spinosaurus thrashed. Jack half expected it to climb back on board. But it didn't.

Next to him, Oliver gripped the box of matches with a shaking hand. "We did it," he murmured.

Jack pulled Oliver close and slapped him on the back. He waited for relief to sweep through him, but none came. "We did." He drew back. "We need to put out the fire."

He forced himself to move to the nearest fire extinguisher. The ship and the people on board were his responsibility. But the responsibility that he'd once craved was now too much. He wanted to sail along the Mediterranean, to show guests the beauty. To live surrounded by the water and wealth.

Now all he had was death and dinosaurs.

He put out the fire with a few careful bursts from the extinguisher.

The water had gone quiet, which was worse. Where had it gone? He made his way over and searched the water for the Spinosaurus, but there was no sign of it. It was gone. If it was dead, it would've sunk to the bottom. That it was alive and pissed off made his stomach knot. Would it stay away or return to finish the job?

"Help me cast us off." He started untying the rope. It would be quicker to cut it, but he didn't want to waste what they had. He looped the rope on the deck in a neat coil that was out of place in the wreckage. The deck was a hazard to anyone walking over it. The splinters could cause a serious injury. At some point, he was going to have to do something about it. But not right now.

"Where are we going?" Oliver dropped his rope. While once Jack would've fixed it up, right now it didn't matter.

While he wanted to believe that there was a safe time to cross the open water, it was a lie he was telling himself and everyone else. "I think we should head out. We either go home—"

"Or we are eaten," Oliver finished.

"I was going to say turn around and find a place to make camp." But Oliver was being more realistic.

"We should take a vote."

Jack nodded. "Get Noah up here. And bring some water."

His throat was like sandpaper, and his head pulsed with every heartbeat. Oliver went below, and for several moments Jack stared at the ruined deck and railing of the ship. At least she was watertight, and the engines still ran. It would get them home, he glanced out at the sea, if that was possible.

He unlocked the bridge and turned on the engines. He checked the gauges, and most importantly the fuel. They had enough to go out and return. He was sure of it. He tried not to look at the first aid kit on the floor, or the blood smear, where he'd spent last night with Emma. But it drew his gaze, and it felt like he couldn't breathe.

Everything had gone wrong, and he didn't know how or why it had happened.

The surface of the water rippled and sparkled beneath the clear and cloudless sky. It was an almost perfect day for being out on the water. If he ignored the fact that the flying creatures weren't birds but dinosaurs, or that they were going to be eaten as soon as they got out into deeper water.

Maybe being eaten wouldn't be so bad. It certainly wouldn't be worse than trying to survive in this piece of forgotten hell.

He sniffed and drew in a breath. Yeah, they'd sail out and keep going until something happened.

Footsteps made him turn.

Noah and Oliver. Their sunny relationship had dissolved, and they both wore scowls. Oliver handed him a bottle of water and a plate of fruit. Emma must have prepared it…

A lump formed in his throat. He took a gulp of water and almost choked on it. He had to keep it together.

"Take us home," Noah said, like that was actually possible.

"Let me adjust the time dial…oh wait, there isn't one."

Noah crossed his arms. "Very funny."

None of this was funny. "If we go out, there's a good chance that we'll die. If something attacks the boat, we could be eaten or drown."

"And if we stay here, it's much the same. I want to go home," Noah said, like he expected Jack to get right to it. While he was pretty and charming when he wanted to be, Jack saw through his smile to the man beneath. Now Oliver did too.

"We all want to go home," Oliver added, "but we don't know how."

That was the problem. They had no idea, and everything they did was a risk, with no promise of success. It was hopeless. Humans were never meant to be here. And dinosaurs weren't meant to be in the Mediterranean either.

How many had swum across to the present…future…and what chaos were they causing?

Was that the reason no one was looking for them?

"Even if we make it, there'll be more dinosaurs on the other side. We have to reach land."

"There'll be other boats out," Noah said, like he knew what was going on.

"Will there?" Oliver glanced at Jack and then at Noah. "How long do we stay out for hoping to sail through to our time?"

Jack studied the gauges for longer than necessary. "If we want to return to land, half an hour. Any longer and we won't make it back."

Noah lifted an eyebrow. "Back here, where there's already two kinds of carnivores that want to eat us?"

"Where would you like me to take you? Coast of France? Greece? This is it for land. I don't want to be adrift out there." Jack flung his arm out, pointing at the sea.

Oliver nodded. "I agree. We go out, see what we can, pray we don't get eaten and that we get home, and if we don't, we come back and find a place to make camp."

"And then what? We'll be out of fuel." Noah's voice rose as panic set in as if until now, he'd believed that they'd be able to go home.

"Then we survive and hope that someone comes looking."

"But what if no one comes?"

"Then…then this is it," Jack said. He wasn't able to keep any kind of hope in his voice.

"And what about Paul?" Noah pressed.

Oliver rounded on his friend. "Now you care? You didn't bother to help last night."

"I was scared."

"So was I."

Jack stepped between them. "If he's dead, we can't help him. If he's alive, then getting home is the best thing we can do."

"And if we can't make it home and he's alive?"

"Then we're going to have to figure out a way to get rid of the dinosaurs by the door and help him."

"With no supplies." Once again, Noah looked unimpressed, like this was all Jack's fault. He hadn't wanted to look at the whale in the first place. He'd wanted to head for shore.

"You'd better hope we get home." Jack returned to the controls. For a heartbeat everything seemed alien, like he'd forgotten how to drive a boat. "We're agreed that we go out, spend half an hour and return."

"Yes," Oliver said.

"Fine." Noah left the bridge and sat outside amongst the devastation.

Oliver hesitated, torn between staying and going outside.

"You might as well sit with him. There's nothing for you to do in here." Jack inclined his head at the door.

"I'm not sure I want to be out there. I don't want to see what's in the water."

CHAPTER 16

Oliver sat with his back to the bridge, the sun on his face and his eyes closed, trying to pretend that they were in the Mediterranean. That Emma would bring out lunch, and Henry and Tahlia would come back from riding the jet skis.

"What are you thinking about?" Noah sat next to him.

He wasn't about to be honest with him. "Stuff."

"Like?"

"Like, how are we going to survive if we can't go home? I don't know how to catch and kill animals. I don't know what plants to eat." He opened his eyes. "But I don't want to die either."

"We should've stayed home and let your brother bring more friends."

"Yeah. But it's too late to go back…" he stopped and laughed. They had gone back in time, just a touch too far.

"What's so funny?"

"That time travel is impossible and yet here we are." He tilted his head back and stared at the pterosaurs circling overhead. Did they think they were dinner or were they curious?

Probably dinner.

"I've been thinking about it. The lights in the sky were from the solar flares—I'd heard a warning that they'd been getting bigger."

"And?"

"They emit a lot of power. Couple that with the recent magnetic fluctuations—"

"And what, an accidental time machine was created?"

Noah shrugged. "Got a better idea?"

"We're dead and in hell?" That was just as plausible, right? He didn't know much about solar flares and magnetic fields.

Noah didn't say anything.

"If we needed a solar flare and magnetic fluctuations to get here, then won't we need the same conditions to get back?"

Noah licked his lips and nodded. "I'm hoping that there is a portal and that it is open. When we arrived, there were lights in the sky. Which means that this time period was experiencing the same things."

"So the portal opened because there was energy on both sides?"

"Something like that," Noah said. "It's only a theory. Don't you watch the news?"

"Yeah…but no one said a portal to the past was a possibility. They said electronics would be affected. This is a bit more serious." Oliver stood. They needed to turn around and head back to shore. Without a miracle, they weren't going anywhere.

The boat rocked as something surfaced near them, and Oliver grabbed for the doorway. The creature was huge. It rolled to look at them with an eye like a dinner plate. Was it curious or hungry? He didn't really want to find out. The creature sunk below.

Noah pointed across the boat. "Is that a shark fin?"

Oliver stared. "Yes."

Clearly sharks had been around forever. And from the size of the fin, it didn't look small. "I think we need to go back to land."

"But the portal we came through might still be here." Noah got up and started scanning the sea. "It can't have closed."

"Why couldn't it have? If it needed freak conditions to be created, how would it stay open?"

"I don't know. But we shouldn't be here. This is all a mistake." Noah's voice rose. "We have to get home."

Oliver shook his head. "There are a lot of giant animals, but no portals. We're stuck here."

"Guys…" Jack called from the bridge. Oliver stepped inside. "I don't think this is such a good idea anymore." Jack pointed out the window. There was more than one shark getting close.

"I feel the same." Knowing that there were big ancient monsters in the sea was very different to seeing them up close. The boat had seemed huge when he'd first gotten on board, now it felt tiny. A kid's toy bobbing in a bath. "Take us to the nearest land."

Everything seemed so far away, and he wasn't even sure they were in the area they'd slipped through. He glanced up at the sky, but there was no sign of the aurora or the solar flares.

"What are you doing?" Noah stood in the doorway, gripping the frame.

"Going back. We are prey and there's nothing out here but water and monsters."

"You don't know that," Noah whined.

"You said yourself there was a massive solar flare. That it was an accidental time machine that we had the misfortune of being caught in," Oliver said. He didn't want to be here, but he wanted to die in the jaws of a sea monster even less.

Something nudged the boat, and his heart almost stopped.

Jack did something, and the boat moved faster. He was no longer cruising to conserve fuel. The engine thrummed beneath them. Shouldn't the creatures be afraid of the noise, and of the new thing? Or were they protecting their territory?

The sharks followed, their fins cutting through the water.

"I didn't travel millions of years back to be eaten by sharks. I could've done that in our own time," Oliver muttered.

Jack laughed. "True."

"You two are mad." Noah shook his head. "Holy shit."

Oliver turned in time to see a mosasaur lurch out of the water and grab a shark in its jaws. His brain went blank. He was so used to thinking of sharks as the biggest predator in the ocean that to see one be eaten so easily...

Noah stepped into the bridge, like the flimsy walls were going to protect him. "Can this go any faster?"

"I'm trying, but if I fuck the engine, we won't be going anywhere and I don't feel like a swim, do you?" Jack snapped. He kept his gaze firmly ahead, but Oliver could see the tension in his shoulders and the way his hand gripped the steering wheel tight enough that the skin of his knuckles was white. "Yell if we're about to be eaten, okay?"

Oliver nodded, and his gaze landed on the flare gun. "How many more flares do we have?"

"Check the box." Jack pointed to the brightly labelled box. "Is it worth putting life jackets on?"

Oliver did as he was asked. "Should we grab the life raft, too?"

"If the monster that ate the shark bites the boat, a blow-up life raft isn't going to do us much good," Noah shouted. "I knew this holiday was too good to be true. I should've never listened to you."

"Same," Oliver said.

Noah glared at him. "What's that supposed to mean?"

Oliver shrugged. "Just that."

He always fell for a pretty smile and there was never anything beneath it. Well, he would never have the chance to mess up his dating life again. Nor would he have to worry about flunking exams or pleasing his father. He studied the ocean behind them. Somewhere out there was the place they'd crossed through. It was a miracle they'd made it to shore in the dark.

"You're breaking up with me? Now?" Noah dragged Oliver's attention away from the water.

"I don't know what I'm doing beyond surviving. Why don't you watch the water?" Oliver opened the box. There were three more flares.

"I don't take orders from you."

"Then take them from me," Jack snapped. "Watch the damn water."

"Fine. Though I don't know why; if we're going to die, do you really want advance notice?"

"Yes," Jack and Oliver said at the same time.

Jack loaded a flare into the gun and handed it to Oliver. "Do you know how to use it?"

"Point and shoot?" It wouldn't do much beyond startling a dinosaur, but if it bought them a few seconds that might be enough.

"Flick the safety off first and don't shoot Noah."

Oliver smiled. "I'll try not to."

Jack glanced at him and nodded. "I hope you don't need to use it."

"Yeah." He stood in the doorway. Noah sat on the deck, flicking splinters of wood away. "I'm sorry for snapping at you."

"No you're not. You're having too much fun showing off for Jack, and being a hero."

Oliver pressed his lips together. It had nothing to do with Jack. "Emma was his girlfriend. He watched her be eaten this morning. We narrowly avoided getting eaten." The whole time, Noah had been hiding. "It would've been nice to have some help."

Noah shook his head. "I'm not that person. You knew that when we got together. I like fun, I don't do drama." He waved his hand in the air. "This is drama."

"This is all we have." The words felt kind of final. Like he'd admitted the truth, that this was his life now. There was no going home.

"How can you be okay with that?" Noah seemed like he was on the edge of breaking.

"I'm not." If a portal opened up in front of him now, he'd be gone in a heartbeat. "But I need to be. You need to be. We need to figure out how we are going to survive, because if we don't, we die. This is it. No rescue is coming. We don't even know how the solar flare affected our time."

Noah tossed another piece of wood away. "This isn't my life."

"It is now."

Something small broke the surface. Then a graceful neck followed. A smile formed on Oliver's lips. "Plesiosaur. I'm pretty sure they're friendly."

"That's about the only thing that is," Noah grumbled.

"Shit." Jack turned the boat hard to the right.

Oliver stumbled and reached for the door frame. Noah slid over the deck toward the broken railing. He grabbed at the deck and held on.

"What the hell!" Oliver shouted. Then he saw it. At first it seemed like an island as big as the boat, but as they moved past it, he realized it was a turtle.

"Hitting that would've wrecked the boat."

"Yeah." Oliver could see how that would be a bad thing. He let himself glance forward and was glad to see land was not that far away. Was the water getting shallower? Did that mean less chompy things that might risk taking a bite out of them?

There were no more shark fins. The turtle sank beneath the water again. And for a few moments he let himself enjoy the salt air and the breeze on his face. They were almost at the coast.

"Oliver, we have a small problem."

He opened his eyes and looked at where Jack was pointing. They were close enough to the shore that he could now see the mangrove trees. Which meant he was close enough to see the Spinosaurs lazing in the shallows like overgrown crocs.

He watched as two of them slid into the water, the sails on their backs cutting toward them. They weren't going to outrun them.

CHAPTER 17

One Spinosaurus on the boat had been bad…but two? The boat would sink or capsize. Either way, the results weren't going to be good for them. Jack watched as they swam swiftly toward the boat.

"Do you think they are friends of the one we set fire to?" Oliver whispered like the beast would overhear.

Jack didn't like the idea that they had friends or that they were smart enough to want revenge. But they had seen the boat and had been a bit too fast to slide into the water and come after them.

"What do you want me to do?" Oliver asked.

What could they do? They had no more fuel lying around. All they had was a flare gun.

"Shoot it in the mouth if it gets too close. Maybe that will deter it." Or it would piss it off. He didn't know. "I'm going to take us away from the swamp."

And hopefully out of its territory. Perhaps that's all it was, protecting territory, not a quest for revenge. That assumed that there wasn't something bigger and badder waiting around the point that would also want to protect its area of coast. And also hoping that the swamp ended and didn't go on forever. Or for as far as their fuel lasted. He didn't fancy hiking through the swamp to dry ground.

All he wanted was a nice river to drive the boat up. That would also give them fresh water and a chance at surviving. At least that's what he was hoping, anyway.

He could be wrong about everything.

Noah was grumbling about moving farther away from where they arrived. He wasn't going to be any help in fighting off dinosaurs. But Oliver had a bit of fight about him that Jack liked, that he needed, because it would be all too easy to quit. With Oliver wanting to fight and live, it forced Jack to get his shit together and do his best. At some point he'd need to stop and grieve and come to terms with everything, but if he did that now he would die. And he wasn't ready to die, even if he wasn't sure how to live.

"They're gaining," Oliver called.

Jack glanced over his shoulder. He could only see one sail, but that was enough to make his heart quicken, and his gut tighten. They were dead if the Spinosaurs reached them. He concentrated on driving, hoping that Oliver was up to the task of keeping the dinosaurs away.

While he didn't want to go back to the open water, being close to the coast had its own problems. There were rocks and trees in the water, and they could be as dangerous as a mosasaur to the boat. Rupturing even one hull would be devastating. He went a little farther out, hoping to deter the Spinosaurs. The boat jerked beneath him and for half a heartbeat he thought he'd hit something.

Noah ran into the bridge. "They're bumping us. Go faster or something."

He was going as fast as he could while still conserving fuel. All he saw was more swamp and nowhere to land the boat. If they ran out of fuel, they'd have to carry what they could and flee through the swamp. And if that happened, they were as good as dead come night. "Look for a river we can turn up."

"A river?"

"Just do as you're asked." The boat lurched again. He turned to search for Oliver, who was still out on the deck. "Are you alright?"

"Yeah. I think they're playing with us, so I don't want to waste the flare."

The boat rocked and lurched and jostled as the dinosaurs became braver, or bored, and wanted their meal.

They rounded the point and, like Jack had feared, there was more mangrove swamp. His heart sank. All his hope had been on getting out of the swamp and finding a beach and river and something more habitable.

"There's more of them." Noah pointed out the broken window.

"I saw." Even through the cracks caused by the tail of the Spinosaurus they'd set fire to, it was clear more of the monsters were sliding out of the tree line and into the water toward them.

The boat lifted and the engine whined before it dropped back into the water. It was only a matter of minutes before they flipped the boat. He'd thought they'd last longer than a day. Maybe a month. Maybe they could go full caveman and make it a decade before succumbing. Why he wanted to live in this nightmare he didn't know, but dying held no allure.

Noah started to cry.

"A river, we need a river, Noah." Jack couldn't drive the boat, watch out for submerged hazards, dinosaurs, and rivers.

"I am looking." Noah scrubbed at his face.

"One of them has disappeared," Oliver called.

That wasn't a good thing. And Jack didn't believe it. "They're smarter than they look."

The bumping continued, then stopped.

Three others were in the water now, but keeping their distance.

"What's happening, Oliver?" Jack shouted. He didn't dare risk looking behind.

"Nothing good."

"What does that mean?" Jack glanced at Noah, but Noah was staring out the shattered window, searching for a river.

"Brace!" Oliver yelled.

For a few seconds, nothing happened. Then something hit the boat, hard. It sunk low in the water. Beyond the cabin, something snapped and growled. They'd been boarded again. This time it was going to be that much harder to get the beast off the boat.

Jack saw the flash of the flare gun reflected on the glass in front of him. It was only then he glanced around, fearing that Oliver was dead, or worse, fatally injured.

Oliver stood on the deck, flare gun in hand.

The Spinosaurus seemed shocked.

And everything was still for a heartbeat.

Then the Spinosaurus started thrashing and clawing at its throat and face. Oliver scrambled out of the way as the beast lashed out.

"Get in here," Jack yelled, not wanting Oliver to be killed but unable to help him.

"There." Noah pointed to what appeared to be a break in the trees. "Is that a river?"

Something slammed into the bridge and the wall Noah had been leaning on crumpled. He flung himself at the other wall like that was more secure. As long as the thrashing dinosaur didn't destroy the actual controls, Jack could deal with rest of the damage.

"I bloody hope so." Not that it would solve their problem, but if they could escape from the pissed off Spinosaurs, it would give them some time to make a plan.

The enraged beast made the boat rock. Things were cracking and breaking. Whatever the flare gun had done to it mustn't be good.

Jack kept his gaze on the break in the trees. "What's going on back there?"

"I don't know," Noah whimpered.

"Have a look!"

Noah edged toward the door. "Um…it's trying to rip its face off."

"Where's Oliver?"

"I can't see him." Noah's voice was high and laced with panic.

"Fuck." But there was nothing Jack could do. He had to drive. "Grab another flare and see if you can find him."

Noah shook his head and clung to the door frame. "I'm not going out there."

The boat tilted so much that Jack fell against the wall of the bridge. His shoulder hit hard, and he let go of the wheel. He reached for the wheel as the boat was knocked again. "If you don't help, we aren't going to get out of this deep water. And if we stay here, they well flip us and eat us. Your choice."

With the jostling, it took all of his effort to keep on course. He was going to have to slow when he reached the gap. If it wasn't a river…

He eased off the throttle. When he glanced around, Noah was gone. He hoped that he was careful and didn't end up falling overboard. If he did, there would be no life ring thrown over for him. There was no one to throw it for a start. And secondly, by the time he threw one, Noah would probably be dead.

***

Oliver crouched by the life raft. His hand was wrapped around the strapping so tight the rope was cutting into his skin. The Spinosaurus that he'd shot in the mouth was lumbering around and lashing out with claws and tail. Blood was smeared on the deck where the dinosaur had raked at its throat.

Oliver had waited, just as Jack had said. The beast had opened its mouth to bite him and he'd fired. For a heartbeat he'd thought he was going to be eaten, but then the flare had exploded, illuminating the back of the monster's throat. And the beast had turned its head like Oliver had smacked it on the snout.

He'd taken that opportunity to run. Oliver was sure the beast could smell him, even if it couldn't see him because it was rather distracted. That didn't calm his pulse or make him feel any better. He longed for the illusion of safety that the bridge offered, even though he knew if he got up and ran, he'd never make it as the beast would be on him in a heartbeat.

The boat bounced like it was going over rapids as the other Spinosaurus played with it. The dinosaurs didn't know what it was, or how it worked, only that there were some creatures on there and they had wounded two of their friends.

The one on the boat gave a choked roar and then a hole appeared in its neck. Blood and spit poured onto the deck. The hole widened.

It took several seconds for Oliver to understand what he was seeing.

But it looked as if the flare had burned a hole through its throat.

The beast convulsed and fell over. Its legs scrabbled against the deck, but there was no more fight. Those were the death throes of a monster.

He'd killed it.

At least he hoped it was dead and that the hole in the throat had killed it because he was not ready for round two.

A tremor filled him. If he looked, his hands would be shaking. He should be glad that it was dead. But his stomach was tight, and he wanted to throw up. The stink of the gore on the deck wasn't helping his unsettled stomach.

Noah stuck his head out of the bridge. He stared at the Spinosaurus as if debating if it was safe to move. Oliver raised his hand so Noah could see him and report that he was alive.

The boat lifted and slapped back down, bouncing the body of the dead dinosaur.

Noah skirted around the dinosaur as though expecting it to get up and run over. He pressed another flare into his hand. "Jack said you might need it."

There were only two flares left, and he didn't want to use them all today. What if there was something bigger out there?

What was he thinking? Of course there was something worse out there. And two tiny flares would only stop two dinosaurs. They weren't worth saving.

"Thanks."

Noah pressed his lips together. "I'm sorry for earlier."

"It's fine." He didn't have the brain to devote to making Noah feel better while they were being thrown around by some pissed off dinosaurs.

Noah opened his mouth.

Oliver shook his head. "Go back to the bridge, and hold on to something, because I don't think they are going to give up."

The boat turned. He hoped that was Jack's doing and not something monster related.

Claws hooked over the side and a snout peered over. Noah gripped Oliver's arm. Oliver shook him off. He had to let go of the strapping to load the flare gun. His hands shook, but he got it done. He was ready for the next one.

But it didn't climb on the way Oliver feared. It snapped at the tail of its dead friend and latched on. They ate each other?

His stomach kicked and he swallowed hard.

Then he watched as the body of the dead Spinosaurus was dragged off the boat, leaving behind a slick red smear. The head got stuck on the damaged railing. As the dinosaur tried to tug it free, the boat rocked.

"What the hell is it doing?" Noah murmured.

"I don't know. Grabbing an easy dinner? Taking the body home to be mourned over?" They looked like monsters, but maybe they got upset about the death of a friend. He didn't want to get to know them well enough to find out.

The boat tilted as the dinosaur pulled. Oliver grabbed for the strap. Noah was too slow. He grabbed onto Oliver's legs and for a moment he dangled there, seconds away from sliding over the deck and into the water where there were at least another three Spinosaurs lurking.

The head came free, and the corpse splashed into the water.

The boat crashed back down.

Water sloshed over the deck, spreading blood and gore over the ripped-up wood. Oliver's clothes were already wet, now they were soaked with blood. He didn't want to smell like blood when surrounded by predators.

Noah was in no better shape. He had blood on his face and arms.

"Go back to the bridge. Now."

This time, Noah got up and ran.

Oliver stayed where he was. He should get up, but he didn't want to move. He was fine sitting here and holding on. He had the flare gun and had killed one big beast. He was a dinosaur hunter.

He kept talking himself up, so he'd feel braver.

The adrenaline that had kept him going was fading fast, leaving him cold and shaky and sick. The rocking stopped. And the open water that had stretched to the horizon had been replaced with trees. He got to his knees and peered back.

The Spinosaurs were tearing apart the dead one, staining the water red as they devoured their fallen comrade.

He glanced to the side and realized the boat was heading up a river.

That had to be safer.

No more open water meant smaller beasts. The mangroves eventually gave way to grasses, and the landscape opened up. Herds of dinosaurs, big ones, plant eaters from the look of them, grazed nearby. Everything here was big. From the animals to the insects to the plants. Some of the giant herbivores lifted their heads as the boat motored by.

An animal with horns stopped drinking to watch. It was easily the size of a four-wheel drive, not including its tail. While it might eat plants, it would do some damage to them if it decided that they were trouble. But the river was wide, and it felt safe to watch the dinosaurs go about their business.

Slowly he got up. He made his way over the deck, trying not to step in the slippery gore. Finally, he reached the bridge. From this vantage point, the river stretched on forever. "How far are we going?"

"I don't know," Jack said. "As far as I can take us?"

"We need somewhere protected. We'll never survive on the plain," Noah added.

"There are orange dinos below deck, and there is blood everywhere. I think we should deal with them before we find somewhere to camp."

Jack nodded. "I can put down an anchor. We might be safe here for a bit."

"No, keep us moving." Oliver didn't want to stop. Stopping might make the non-friendly ones think they were worth investigating. "At least until we've cleaned off the deck."

"There are cleaning things below, in the cupboard marked staff." Jack turned and glanced over his shoulder. "Are you sure you're okay to do that?"

"Yeah." No, but he was less okay with drawing predators to their campsite. "Noah?"

Noah nodded and followed Oliver. Oliver put the flare gun in his pocket and went down the ladder. He only made it halfway before one of the orange things ran at him. He yelped and drew his legs up. The things snapped and snarled and kicked.

Noah watched through the hatch. "How are we supposed to get rid of them?"

CHAPTER 18

Oliver didn't have an answer for Noah, but he needed to come up with one fast. They needed access to the cleaning supplies, the kitchen, and their cabins. And they needed to find out if Paul was alive.

The only reason the orange things were still there was because they clearly couldn't climb a ladder. There was a door in the galley to the lower deck where the lounge area and jet skis were.

"Noah, grab a chunk of Spinosaurus off deck, then open the door to the dining room, drop it and run."

"What are you going to do?"

"Hope they smell the meat and help herd them if they don't move." He glanced over his shoulder. "And tell Jack to shut the door to the bridge in case they look for more to eat."

He watched as Noah disappeared from view.

He had no idea how he was going to herd them, but they'd chase him and that might be good enough. He crouched and closed the hatch so they couldn't accidentally fall back down. Then waited, hunched on the top couple of steps, for the door in the galley to open. The stink of blood and his own sweat filled his lungs in the cramped space.

A pack of the orange dinosaurs snapped at the lower rungs, all jostling for position and first bite. Once the door opened and they moved, he wouldn't have long. But if he could reach the cupboard and grab a mop or a broom, or something…

Irritation burned in his veins. What was taking Noah so long?

He was about to open the hatch and call out when he heard a door open. The dinosaurs heard it too. Their heads tilted and their nostrils flapped. They smelled something. Whether it was the dead Spinosaurus or Noah, Oliver didn't know.

However, it took the dinosaurs several seconds before they started moving, slowly at first, toward the galley. He hoped Noah had gotten out of the way. If not, they were going to be all over him. With the dinosaurs distracted, Oliver climbed down and ran for the cupboard. It wasn't locked.

He yanked it open and grabbed the first thing with a long handle that he saw. He turned, as a dinosaur kicked at him. He smacked it away with the mop and sent it skittering along the corridor in the wrong direction.

Damn.

Checking over his shoulder that the rest had gone out, he retreated to the galley, and then to the dining room. The other dinosaurs were on the deck arguing over the chunk of meat. His grip on the mop tightened. They couldn't be left on the deck as they'd take over, making movement impossible. They needed to be removed.

He glanced at the mop. Then at the dinosaurs. He could do this.

He stepped out and rushed the first one he saw, sweeping it off the deck and into the water. Standing near the edge, he let the others come to him and batted them in as fast as they ran at him, but the last two were much more cautious.

"What do you want me to do?" Noah called from the upper area.

Not distract me.

Oliver tried a few times to sweep the remaining two off, but they were smart, and they didn't want to end up in the river. He didn't blame them. But this wasn't their boat.

He glanced at Noah. "Go down the hatch, close it after you, and grab another mop, or something. There's another dino inside so be careful." With two of them, they stood a chance.

He knew Noah had been successful when the last remaining one came running out of the dining room. Oliver didn't give it a chance to hear the gossip from its buddies. He knocked it off the side and watched it flounder. It didn't struggle for long. Something toothy surfaced and grabbed it. Then the surface of the river was still.

Noted: no swimming in the river.

Noah held the broom like it was going to bite him.

The two remaining dinos watched them and chatted to each other. No doubt they were planning.

"Shut the door," Oliver said. The dinosaurs were not getting back inside, no matter what.

Two dinos, two humans. That seemed like good odds.

"What now?" Noah stood near the door with the broom held out, like he expected the remaining two orange ones to attack him.

They wouldn't, not yet anyway because they were too busy watching Oliver. He'd attacked four of them, and he was the dangerous one. He didn't take his gaze off them. If they both attacked him, he was going to have a hard time defending himself, and the last thing he wanted was to fall overboard.

"We're cleaning the decks. Just use the broom and help me push them off." Oliver took a step toward them. They shuffled sideways like they had learned what would happen if they fell over.

Oliver understood their fear. He had no desire to go over either. Noah walked closer, but stayed behind Oliver.

"I need you next to me. We have to work together to herd them." Oliver made a feint to the left to see what they'd do. They scuttled right. They weren't going backwards. These two were going to be much harder to deal with than the others.

Noah didn't move. "They'll bite us."

"It's their toe claws you have to worry about." Their teeth were small in comparison. "On three, we rush forward. If they run at you, pretend you're playing cricket."

"I never played cricket."

"Hockey, whatever. Just whack them and try to sweep them off the boat." Oliver opened his mouth to start counting.

"It's pointless. More dinosaurs will come and investigate."

Oliver huffed out a breath. "One. Two." He wasn't waiting for Noah. The longer they spent in this weird standoff the harder it was going to be. He was sure the dinosaurs sensed Noah's hesitation, or smelled his fear or something. As he said three, he knew they were going to go for Noah, the weakest.

Oliver yelled and ran toward them.

The two dinosaurs ducked right and ran at Noah, who was rooted to the spot. Oliver spun.

"Don't just stand there!" Oliver caught the tail of one with the mop. It turned and snapped at it, grabbing hold of the end. Oliver swung the mop up and brought it down over the side of the boat. The dinosaur dangled over the water. Its eyes widened.

Its dangerous, hooked claws scrabbled at the air. Oliver shook the mop, then he slammed it against the side of the boat. It took three goes before the dinosaur let go and fell into the water.

"Look out!" Noah shouted.

Oliver turned as the last orange dinosaur attacked him. It lashed out, kicking and clawing, until Oliver was closer to the edge than he wanted to be. In the water there were fish that were bigger than him feeding on the dinosaurs he'd been throwing overboard. He had no doubt the fish, and whatever else lived in the river, would be more than happy to give human a try.

All he could do was use the mop to stab downward and keep it back. He needed to move away from the edge of the boat, but every time he tried to make a break, the dinosaur copied. It had watched and learned and was extremely pissed off from the noises it was making and the way its spiky feathers were standing on end.

"A little help?" Oliver didn't look up and didn't know where Noah was.

All he was doing was enraging the critter more. It wasn't afraid of the mop. Just like playing cricket is what he'd told Noah. A smile formed. There were two sides to a boat, and he didn't have to push it off the closest side.

Oliver turned sideways, like he was standing at the crease. He tapped the mop on the deck. "Come on, fucker, give it to me."

The dinosaur didn't hesitate. It was like it saw the lowered mop as weakness or surrender. Oliver swung the mop back as it ran toward him, leaving it a clear opening as it lifted its leg to kick. As the dinosaur went airborne, Oliver swung like he had to hit a six to win the game.

The mop and dinosaur connected with a sickening crunch. The dinosaur soared into the air like an orange ball, over the boat, and into the river with a splash. The resulting feeding frenzy was better than the roar of the crowd.

He gave himself a fist pump. "Did it." Then he lowered the mop and stared at Noah. "What the hell?"

"I didn't know what to do. They look at me and I freeze. They're fucking dinosaurs!"

"Yeah, and you'd better get used to it. Because this is where we live now." He hated he was saying that, because saying it out loud made it real. And the last thing he wanted was to spend his days being the first caveman to ever walk the Earth.

CHAPTER 19

With the orange dinosaurs removed from the ship, Oliver went inside to assess the damage. The supplies in the galley seemed to be untouched—which gave them some food to start with, but it wouldn't be long until they needed to figure out how to hunt and gather. The moment he started thinking of the future, his mind locked up, like it couldn't process what was happening.

He pushed aside thoughts of survival. They were fine for the moment. They had food and water and were cruising up a river that wasn't filled with Spinosaurs. That was the first win they'd had since the whale had been attacked.

Below deck there was dino shit and piss, blood smears and claw marks. The cabin doors were all closed, which meant that at least they had bedding and clothes and a safe place to sleep.

All that was left was to find out if Paul was dead or alive.

He didn't know what he was hoping for. He didn't want to wish him dead, but to be alive and suffering, and then not having access to doctors or medicine?

Oh God.

They didn't have access to medicine.

What if he got an infected cut? Or appendicitis or broke a leg?

All the things he'd taken for granted back home, he suddenly wanted really badly. Everything from clean water, to grabbing a burger, to having a house and car. While the boat seemed safe, it was already damaged, and they'd only been here twenty-four hours.

He kept hold of the mop in case there was another of the nasty little dinosaurs hiding in the corridors, but when he stepped around, there was nothing but blood and a few feathers.

The door handle to the bathroom was smeared with blood, and the surface of the door was covered in scratches. In some places the outer surface of the door had been ripped away. They'd been so close to breaking in...

He hesitated, not sure what to do, then knocked. As soon as he'd done it, it seemed like a dumb thing to do. It's not like Paul was taking a shower or using the toilet. Oliver rested the mop to the side and carefully cracked open the door—he didn't want to open it into Paul's head.

After a few inches there was resistance, but there was enough room for him to see it was only Paul's legs in the way.

"Paul?" There was a lot of blood on the floor. And tiny footprints.

As his brain registered what that meant, an orange dinosaur ran at him. Oliver slammed the door, trapping the dino in the frame. It kicked and squawked. Oliver stepped back to avoid its claws while keeping hold of the door handle. If he let go, he was fucked.

"Noah!"

No answer.

He pulled on the door, trying to squash the thing. Could he reach the mop? And do what, poke it?

What he needed was for it to latch on like the other one. Keeping one hand on the handle he reached out for his new favourite household object—he'd never mopped a floor in his life but for attacking dinosaurs it was perfect.

He jabbed the mop at it, and the snarly thing latched on. Oliver slammed it against the wall, and then the opposite wall. The dinosaur fell off and lay motionless on the floor. Oliver gave it a poke, expecting it to jump up, but it stayed down.

It was only then he sighed with relief.

Once again, he approached the bathroom door. This time, nothing ran at him. He pushed into the bathroom and scanned the room, but nothing moved.

Not even Paul.

Oliver looked away, his throat tight and hot. Paul's face had been chewed off, his fingers were missing, and there was nothing left of his throat. It wasn't even worth checking for a pulse.

He backed out of the room and shut the door. Then he stood there, not sure what to do. They couldn't leave Paul there. He'd rot and attract predators.

They were going to have to bury him.

And not at their new campsite.

He made his way back to the galley. Noah was making lunch.

"Paul's dead."

Noah nodded, as if Oliver had commented on the weather.

"I was attacked…I called for you."

"I know." He lifted his gaze. His eyes were rimmed with red. "I can't do this."

"You don't have a choice." None of them did. "I'm going up to the bridge. Are you going to bring that up? Do you want me to carry anything?"

"No, wash your hands or something and I'll see you up there."

Oliver looked at his hands. He used the galley sink, aware that when they ran out of soap, there'd be nothing to sanitize their hands with and then made his way upstairs.

Jack glanced over his shoulder as Oliver entered.

"All the dinosaurs are off the boat. Paul's dead." Oliver slumped onto the other chair, feeling like he'd run a marathon. All he wanted to do was rest. "Noah's bringing some lunch up."

Jack blew out a breath. "We're running out of fuel."

For several breaths Oliver didn't say anything. What could he say? It's not like they could nip to the service station and top up the tank. "What happens then?"

"We walk, or we stay with the boat and turn it into some kind of shelter."

Oliver stared out the door to the ruined, blood coated deck. "There's too much blood and death."

"Yeah, that's what I was thinking." Jack was grim. "But I don't want to be without shelter. What we need is a cave."

A cave that wasn't already inhabited. "Will we find one of them by the river?"

"I don't know."

Between the three of them, they didn't know anything.

EPILOGUE

From the edge of the cliff, Jack stared out at the sea. The sea was the same as every other day, wide and empty of any human life. Whatever had happened that day they seemed to be the only ones sent back millions of years.

He added a few more words, using up the last of the paper. The pen had run out months ago, and the pencil was now nothing but a nub. But with no more paper to write on, it didn't matter.

One year.

It was longer than he thought they'd survive.

He scratched the beard that now coated his jaw. Hopefully they'd manage a few more. It had taken them a month to find this place. And while there were still dinosaurs, they left each other alone. They were far enough away from the plains that the bigger predators didn't bother them. They had water and Oliver had figured out how to hunt some of the small mammals. He hoped they didn't kill the one that would eventually give rise to humans, but if they did, they figured they'd cease to exist so it wouldn't really matter.

With one final look, he turned away.

Oliver waited by the large pyre they'd built in case someone showed up. A necklace with the claw from one of the orange dinosaurs hung around his neck. His expression was grim behind his dark beard, and he wore his hair long in one braid. Oliver had gotten harder as the months had slid by. His body was all lean muscle. Jack couldn't imagine being stranded without him. He was sure he'd have died without Oliver's grit.

He brushed past him, letting his hand drift over Oliver's lower back. "Light it up."

When they'd first found this place, they'd agreed that when they reached the one-year anniversary of the stranding, they'd drink the rum Jack had found in the bridge and finish the chocolate. They might as well burn the signal fire too. No one was coming.

"You sure?"

A part of him wanted to keep hoping. But it was time to move on. "Yeah. You?"

Oliver nodded. He took the ember out of the container and fanned it to life. The dry wood caught quickly, sending smoke up into the air. They still had emergency matches and a lighter, but where possible they kept an ember alive.

Jack cracked open the little bottle of rum and took a drink before handing it to Oliver.

Oliver took a swig, coughed, and handed it back. "I expected it to be better."

Jack grinned. After a year without alcohol, it was only going to take a little to get him drunk. He wasn't going to drop his guard that much. They couldn't afford to in this place.

They sat and ate the chocolate and watched the flames.

Oliver sighed and rested his head on Jack's shoulder. "I expected more…but it's just another day, isn't it? Nothing special."

Oliver was right. Today didn't mean anything. They'd kept count because a year had once meant something. Here it meant nothing. The turn of the seasons, and the migration pattern of various animals were more important.

"Shall we go home?" Jack stood and offered Oliver his hand.

Oliver accepted, and they walked hand in hand along the trail they'd worn to the cliff edge, passing the markers they'd made for Emma and Paul. Six months ago, they'd buried Noah. He'd tried, but his heart wasn't in survival, and he'd lived in a constant state of panic before ending it.

In the cave, Jack wrapped the notebook in plastic and buried it. Maybe someone in the future would find it and they'd have a warning that something was going to happen. If the people in the future knew what had happened to them, then maybe they'd be rescued.

Or they'd be told not to sail.

He packed down the dirt, waiting to wake up back home or for something about their lives to change. In that same heartbeat, he knew he didn't want to lose Oliver. He lifted his gaze to watch the man who'd become his lover. He waited a few more heartbeats.

Then he stood.

Around him, the cave was filled with drawings and carvings. Anyone who found it would have to realize they hadn't been done by a primitive human.

They'd carved cars and planes, their boat and their names into the walls. They'd written the date of the solar flare and drawn it, too. He'd written about it all in the notebook.

All in the hope that it would be found. That they wouldn't be forgotten.

Oliver studied him. "We're still here."

Jack pressed his lips together. He hadn't changed the future or the past.

All he had was now.

Check out other great

Dinosaur Thrillers!

Doug Goodman

HUNTING WITH DINOSAURS

A hunting party is sent to catch and kill raptors that have escaped Dinosaur Falls Restricted Area and murdered nearby hikers. But the hunters find the raptors are unlike any creature they've ever hunted, and soon one lone bowhunter is running for his life through the Perdidos Mountains. He discovers an old wilderness survival trench and burrows in deep, but eventually the raptors come for him. His only salvation is to befriend a wolf hellbent on destroying the raptors. If they can come together, they can form a pack the world has never seen, but if they fail, the raptors are waiting with their sharp teeth and elongated claws...

Edward J. McFadden III

DINOSAUR RED

There's a doorway on Mars that has mankind's greatest minds perplexed. Deep beneath Aeolis Mons an ancient secret is revealed, and a team of explorers led by Forest Judge, Deputy Commander of Gale Base Alpha, are dispatched to investigate. The prehistoric gateway reveals a biosphere preserving Earth's distant past, and as Judge and crew stand on the threshold of mankind's greatest discovery the Martian ground trembles. A roar thunders from within, the doorway closes, and the team is trapped. Six mission specialists, each with unique skills, each with different reasons for wanting to break free of the primordial trap. To get home Judge is forced to choose between escape and changing the course of humanity. What will he do?

Check out other great

Dinosaur Thrillers!

P.K. Hawkins

THE LOST ISLAND

Scientists Dr. Eccleston and Dr. Lerner have done many routine expeditions for the Skurzon Corporation in the past, helping the company search the ocean for newly available resources freed by melting ice. They're expecting to maybe find oil at the bottom of the Arctic Sea. What they aren't expecting is a lost island that defies all scientific understanding. When something comes out of the sea and destroys their research vessel, the scientists and the rest of the crew are forced into a game of survival against forces no human being has ever seen alive. If they can survive the giant insect swarms, the man-eating plants, and the dinosaurs, they might be able to live to tell the tale. But when each passing moment reveals murderers in their midst, their survival starts to look less and less likely.

William Meikle

THE LAND BELOW

A treasure hunt into the deepest cave system in Europe takes a turn for the worst.Now rather than treasure it is survival that is at the forefront of the spelunkers' thoughts. But their attempt to escape out of the dark deep places is thwarted. Men are not at home in the depths. But there are things that are, pale terrifying things. Huge things.Things red in tooth and claw.

Check out other great

Dinosaur Thrillers!

Gustavo Bondoni

TEST SITE HORROR

Lieutenant Max Alexeyev is a Russian Special Forces soldier. His job is to protect his country's interests at home and abroad, not to rescue overly ambitious reporters who have bitten off stories too big to chew. But when his unit gets called to a press event at a laboratory that has been invaded by dinosaurs, that's exactly what he finds himself doing. Fighting both prehistoric nightmares and the products of modern genetic experiments in the forests of the Ural Mountains, he battles for his own survival as well as that of alluring journalist Marianne Caruso and her peers.Unbeknownst to him, however, shadowy human forces are at work to ensure that no one spills the secrets of the research being done in the area.Will they live to tell the story of the Test Site Horror?

John Lee Schneider

AGE OF MONSTERS

Once upon a time, Dinosaurs ruled the Earth.But the Mesozoic era – the Age of Reptiles – came to its cataclysmic end sixty-five million years ago.The Age of Monsters begins tonight.And the world of humankind will crumble. Some will call it Judgment. Some will attempt to fight. Others will simply run. Most will just try and survive. But no one will escape.In the mountains. In the oceans. In the cities and towns. Even up in space.Where were YOU when the world ended?

Made in United States
North Haven, CT
19 April 2024

51537378R00078